She knew he'd threatened to do this, but she'd thought he was bluffing...he couldn't be serious, could he?

"I need to talk to you," Thomas said to Isabel as she snapped her guitar case closed.

She stood up. Everyone else had filed out but she wasn't afraid of Thomas. Not this time. She waited for him to say whatever he needed to say to make himself feel good about himself—jabs at her singing, insults about her playing. Instead of saying anything, though, he took a manila folder from his bag and slid it across the piano toward her. She looked at him as she caught it and opened it. Only a few words stood out on the paper before her.

Hereby terminated.
With immediate effect.
Rights of two songs retained.
Creative differences.
Settlement.

Isabel's hands shook. Each phrase on the paper before her was a stab in her solar plexus. She could feel Thomas looking at her. She could feel the silence in the room deep in her ears. When she looked up at him, he raised his eyebrows. She could feel bile rise in her throat and had to run across the hall to the bathroom. She barely made it. When she came out of the bathroom after splashing water in her face, he was standing with his arms folded, looking at her as if she were vermin.

Gifted musician and singer Isabel Carson gets an unexpected phone call, asking her to come back for a reunion tour with a band she played for several years ago. Although she has serious reservations, Isabel reluctantly agrees…mainly because she can't pass up the opportunity to see Spencer Logan, the man she loves, one last time. Six years ago, Isabel's relationship with Spencer was sabotaged by Thomas, the jealous and possessive lead singer, and both men hurt her badly. However, once the band is reunited, it doesn't take long for Isabel to realize she's made a terrible mistake. Some things cannot be forgiven, and she would have been better off to have left the past in the past, where it belongs—especially since Isabel now hides a painful secret, one that, if exposed, could destroy what little peace and happiness she's managed to achieve.

KUDOS for *Winter Rain*

In *Winter Rain* by Tanya Newman, Isabel is a singer who takes a position with a band run by Thomas. Thomas wants her, but she falls for his friend and fellow band member Spenser, a fact that brings out the worst in Thomas. Though he claims Isabel as his girlfriend, making it a condition of her joining the band, he cheats on her and, when she breaks up with him, stalks her. It's Spenser she wants and Spenser wants her, but Thomas conspires to keep them apart. He takes his jealousy out on Isabel, destroying more than her career. The book is a fine addition to Newman's repertoire. Well written, poignant, and heartbreaking as well as heartwarming, it gives us a glimpse into the life of a performer that has a definite ring of truth. ~ *Taylor Jones, The Review Team of Taylor Jones and Regan Murphy*

Winter Rain by Tanya Newman is the second novel for this talented author. In this story, a young singer Isabel applies for a position with a band, and is given the job on the condition that she go out with the leader Thomas. Isabel doesn't know if he is joking or serious, but she is afraid to turn him down, just in case, even though she is attracted to Spenser, another member of the band. Although Isabel tries to like Thomas and ignore Spenser, it is impossible for her to do. Spenser cares for her too, and a relationship slowly develops as the two become friends and Isabel falls in love with him. But Thomas is vindictive and spiteful, and even though he cheats on Isabel, causing her to break up with him, he doesn't want her to find love and happiness with Spenser. The old "If I can't have her, no one can" syndrome. *Winter Rain* is not only a love story, it's a story of how cruel people can be to each other. It also spotlights, very realistically, the difficult and often tragic life of entertainers. A really fine read. ~ *Regan Murphy, The Review Team of Taylor Jones and Regan Murphy*

ACKNOWLEDGMENTS

As with all my works, this one would not be here without the help and support of so many people, and I send my thanks and my love to you all:

To God, for giving me the ideas and inspiration to write this story and the drive to keep writing.

To my husband, Mark, for the endless hours you spent talking with me about and designing beautiful covers for my work that capture just what I want and for always discussing new stories with me.

To my mom, for your tireless help and support in getting my work out there in the world and for the weekend trips to Laurens that always seem to inspire a new story!

To my dad, for providing the means to study what I love so that I could do what I love.

To Lauri, Faith, Arwen, and Jack at Black Opal Books for reading my work, for loving it, and for making it better with your stellar editing.

To Marilyn Knight and Keith Lee Morris, for still reading every work I send to you and for making me a better writer.

To Connor and Lydia, for making me a better person each day.

Lastly, to you, for reading my work. Because of your support, I get to keep doing the work I love.

Winter Rain

TANYA W. NEWMAN

A Black Opal Books Publication

Black Opal Books

BECAUSE SOME STORIES JUST HAVE TO BE TOLD

GENRE: ROMANTIC THRILLER/ROMANTIC SUSPENSE/WOMEN'S
FICTION

WINTER RAIN
Copyright © 2017 by Tanya Newman
Cover Design by Mark Newman
All cover art copyright © 2017
All Rights Reserved
Print ISBN: 978-1-626946-69-9

First Publication: MAY 2017

Published by Black Opal Books **http://www.blackopalbooks.com**

DEDICATION

To Barbara

Chapter 1

March 2010:

She could hear him calling to her from far away as she lay at the bottom of the stairs, but she couldn't answer. When she tried to speak, she coughed up a metallic fluid that ran out the side of her mouth. Her chest hurt. It felt a like a balloon whose air was slowly being sucked away. She coughed again. Her chest hurt again. But that's not what troubled her as she heard the nine-one-one operator calling to her again, asking where she was, what had happened.

No, what troubled her most was the pain lower down in her abdomen, pain that spread to her back and legs—

aching, cramping, stabbing. She tried to groan in agony but could only cough up blood again. She was going to die. Right here, like this, with a stranger who didn't even know her name calling out to her.

His was the last voice she would hear, the last thing she was aware of before everything faded away to darkness.

Chapter 2

December 1, 2016:

Thomas knew he was in trouble the second the phone rang. Call it a premonition, a psychic vision brought on by years of failure in the music industry after years of success, whatever. It wasn't good, and he knew it.

"Can you be in by ten?" Gerard asked.

Thomas never heard from Gerard, not directly anyway. He was president of Mystic Records, the independent label Thomas had signed with just last year. Gerard had more important matters on his plate than dealing with musicians directly. Unless it was to drop them.

"Yeah, sure," Thomas said. He replaced his cell on his nightstand, lay back, and rubbed his throbbing temples.

"Who was that?" a cranky voice called from the floor.

"Huh?" Thomas said, sitting up.

Adrienne's blonde curls popped up from the other side of the bed. She stood up, his comforter wrapped around her otherwise naked body. She was the only stripper at the club last night who'd taken him up on his offer of coming back to his place.

Oh, man, Thomas thought, dropping back onto the bed.

"I fell off the bed when the phone rang." Adrienne giggled. She took her half-full wine glass from the night before and downed it.

Geez, Thomas thought.

"Mind if I use your shower, love?"

Thomas didn't answer, just waved her in the direction of the bathroom. Adrienne hopped onto the bed and ran across it to get to the bathroom.

"Hey!" he said, beginning to really regret bringing her home just so he wouldn't have to sleep alone yet again. "There's a perfectly good floor."

Adrienne just giggled again in response. Thomas shook his head and looked at the clock. Already after nine. He'd better get a move on. He threw on a T-shirt and his jeans from last night, grabbed his wallet and cell phone, and threw on his jacket, not bothering to look in the mirror whatsoever. If Gerard was dropping him, Thomas wasn't going to bother getting prettied up. Hell, maybe the homeless look would win him some sympathy points.

Thomas sighed as he sat back down on his bed to put on his boots. No. He knew the only thing that would convince Gerard to keep him on his label. And he knew Gerard was probably going to bring it up yet again, just like he had four times over the past year. Thomas kept refusing, insisting he could gather a following solo. But it hadn't happened. Gerard had given him a year, and it hadn't happened. No one was following him. The only way he would be able to keep making music, keep doing the only thing he knew how to do, the only thing his musician parents had groomed him to do, was to get together the other four singers and musicians who had helped give him the greatest success of his life. Greg and Renee wouldn't be a problem, he knew. But they wouldn't be enough. Without Spencer and without Isabel—Thomas could feel his face tick when he thought of them—there was no band. The only problem was, Spencer hated Thomas, Thomas hated Spencer, and Isabel hated them both.

It was going to take some major thinking to come up with a proposition that would be good enough to even tempt them both.

Thomas opened the door to the bathroom and told

Adrienne to lock up when she left, that he had a meeting to get to. She opened the door to the shower, giving him a full eye's view of her remarkable figure.

"Sure you don't want to join me?" she asked, throwing in a little pout for good measure.

Thomas looked at her for a moment then back at his clock. What the hell? He could probably use the inspiration before going to the biggest meeting of his career.

♫♫♫

Isabel was nearly asleep when the phone rang at midnight. She'd been in bed, dozing against the pillows on her double bed while an episode of *I Love Lucy* played on the classic TV channel. Though her cell phone emitted little more than a faint buzz, she jumped. She supposed it was from living alone for so long. She heard and saw every little thing. She reached over and picked up her phone. She didn't recognize the number, not that anyone she knew should be calling her at that hour, and instead of pressing the "answer" button, continued to look at the number with a grimace until her phone switched to telling her she had a missed call. It had to be a wrong number, she thought. Nonetheless, curiosity got the better of her and she hit the search engine to do a search for the number when her phone dinged, telling her she had one new voicemail.

Fully awake now, Isabel sat up, switched to her voicemail, and hit the number so she could listen. She knew the voice from the first word and sat, motionless, as she listened. No, it wasn't a wrong number. It was a man who knew exactly who he was calling.

"Isabel, it's Thomas." There was a lengthy pause. Isabel was still frozen. "I just…listen, I know I'm probably the last person on earth that you want to hear from, but do you think maybe you could call me? I know it's late and I'm sorry."

He left his number, apologized again, and said he hoped he would hear from her soon. He hadn't given a reason for his call, but as Isabel watched her phone switch back to the screensaver that reminded her of the date and time, she knew exactly why he was calling.

Isabel lay back down. She looked at the ceiling for a long time, throughout the remainder of *Lucy*, then *Gilligan's Island*, then *Petticoat Junction*, before finally pushing the covers aside, draping her robe over her body, and padding to her kitchen to make coffee. Sleep was way too much to hope for right then.

When the coffee was finished, she took her cup to her seat in the bay windows that overlooked the town square so she could think about when she might call him, if she even decided to, and what she would say when she did. She hadn't lived in her hometown of Laurel Springs for almost six years now, but this tiny seaside town of Lilac Cove reminded of her of it all the time. She leaned her head against the window and looked up at the night sky, as dark as the night she'd first set foot in Thomas's apartment, as dark as the night he'd become a murderer.

♬♬♬

A few hours later and clear across the state, Spencer Logan stepped out the back door of the tiny three-room apartment above the coffee shop he'd played in before buying it when Hank, the previous owner, passed away nearly three years ago.

Spencer took the steps quickly down the back, not bothering to warm up as he started a slow, easy gate. It was cold, a little too cold for November, and especially for the small South Carolinian town of Laurel Springs. No one was out at the five a.m. hour, he couldn't help noticing, as he turned onto the town square his coffee shop bordered.

A dense fog had crept in, leaving the brick-faced shops and restaurants that bordered the stone courthouse shrouded in thick, silent gray. Only the moon glowing overhead and the black iron lampposts that ran along the sidewalk provided the little light at that time of the day. He made it to the end of the square and hung a left onto North Harper Street, passed the old Laurel Springs cemetery whose iron gates were shut tight, and turned left again into Laurel Park. He was just slowing his pace when he started to cross Dagnall Bridge, a small brick affair that curved over the Little River, when his phone started buzzing in his pocket. He retrieved it and answered, half out of breath, without first checking who was on the other end.

He wished he had, though, when the person on the other line spoke.

"Spence?"

Spencer stopped breathing, stopped moving altogether. The man on the other end didn't have to say another word for Spencer to know who he was.

"What do you want, Thomas?" he asked the former friend he hadn't spoken to in years, though he already had a pretty good idea of why he was calling.

"Well, I have an offer to make you," Thomas said, delving right in. "You probably know it's the ten year anniversary of our first album."

Spencer knew. He said nothing. Thomas continued.

"Hope—that's our new manager—she thinks it's a good idea to do a reunion, of sorts, of all the past and present members. There'd be a tour, interviews, and, if you're interested, of course, maybe a new album."

He waited for Spencer to respond. When he didn't, Thomas continued.

"She thinks it'd be a good idea to do it in Laurel Springs. I know it's a small town, but I understand you're living there?"

Spencer still said nothing.

"Yeah, that's where we really got started, where we recruited—"

Spencer knew exactly who they'd recruited in Laurel Springs.

"So, think about it, if you don't mind. I know you've been under the radar all these years. I'll give you a call in a few days."

Spencer hung up without saying goodbye and stood there on that bridge long after he'd caught his breath. He looked at the fog all around him, the sapphire blue of the sky as it lightened overhead, and almost forgot where he was.

Chapter 3

September 2009:

Thomas had stared at Isabel for a long time after hearing her sing that afternoon. But instead of offering her the job to play with his band, Shiloh Ridge, he invited her to a party that evening at the second-floor apartment he was renting while his band put together and recorded their latest album.

Isabel knew the reason he told her to come to this party. It was so the rest of the band members could size her up, she thought. She knew the drill. They'd all meet her, assess her, see if she was the right fit. This was an interview as much as it was a social gathering. She knew that. But she also knew there was still hope. As the lead singer, if Thomas already liked her, she'd already won half the battle. She tried to keep that in mind as she knocked on his door, already sweating, even though she hadn't set foot in the overwhelming crowd, hadn't had to try to mingle with a hot flushed face, or come up with something witty to say as her heart slammed against her chest. It wasn't hard doing that when she was writing her songs, even singing those songs in front others in smoke-filled cafes or bars. That was actually the easy part, probably because she'd rehearsed those words, didn't have to come up with something spur of the moment, and could simply slip away when she was done.

She tried to keep all of this, her little talent, her hard-won battle with Thomas, in her mind as he opened the door. He didn't smile when he saw her, but he hadn't smiled at all during her audition in which he made her play not only her acoustic guitar, but two songs on the piano and another on bass.

"Hey," he said. "Come on in."

The apartment was smoky and loud with the slow, easy rock song bellowing from the speakers. People were everywhere, standing in groups or sitting in deep, comfy couches or armchairs, already talking, clutching drinks, and it was hard for Isabel to know where to make a move. Thomas put a hand on her back as he closed the door, leaned in close to her ear.

"Drinks are in the kitchen. Help yourself."

She tried to smile, feeling the tremble and heat in her face. She knew, later that evening, that she'd be exhausted to the point where she'd be asleep before her head hit the pillow. That was the curse of the introvert. Her hands were shaking as she went to the kitchen and selected and opened a bottle of Heineken.

Breathe, she reminded herself, turning around to face the crowd, but her body barely listened. Her eyes scanned the different crowds of two or three people here and there and a couple met her eyes, but didn't pause long enough to welcome her into any conversation or even make room. She kept moving so as not to seem awkward, and before she knew it, she'd moved to the end of the room, to where the French doors stood open, leading to a terrace with wrought-iron railings. There were only a couple of people out there, standing and talking, or smoking. They didn't smile or make eye contact with her, either, so she moved to the other end, looked at the buildings in the distance, the traffic below, breathed in the cool September night air. It was cloudy, and she could already smell rain coming.

This was a bad idea.

Thomas was going to reject her on the simple reason that she didn't fit in, just like she didn't with anyone, any band she auditioned for. She was just a solo singer, a solo person, always would be.

She shrugged to herself, smirked. What else was new? She would go back to the little cafe she'd been playing in for the past month. It was small, cozy, felt good and safe. She actually made decent enough money, and the owner let her rent the little loft over it for just three hundred a month. So, she stood there on that balcony, relaxed, closed her eyes, and enjoyed the cold night air around her.

It was only when she opened her eyes that she saw him there, standing beside her. She half jumped, startled by his presence. He was leaning his back against the railing, his hands in his pockets, just looking but not staring at her with eyes the color of a flame's lowest point. His dark hair was long, past his shoulders, a thick, shaggy, beautiful mess. He half-smiled, but still said nothing as he looked at her.

Then something unlocked in her mind. He had followed her, she suddenly realized, from a distance as she got a beer, as she scanned one crowd at the party, then another, as she went out on the balcony to take in the night sky. He was there, in every moment, but it was like she was just now noticing it.

And it was now, in this moment, that she said to him those first words, asked him that first question: "Do you love me or something?"

It was stupid, she realized, starting with something like that. Even *she* was caught off guard when she asked it. When he didn't answer her question right away, she half-laughed and followed, by way of explanation, with, "Is that why you keep following me?"

She didn't mean to seem unkind. She wasn't accustomed to being so, but neither was she accustomed to being followed.

He took his time answering. He was leaning against the railing, still looking her way. The wind blew his hair away from his face. His eyes warmed as he leaned in close. "Now, you don't have to ask me questions you already know the answer to."

Isabel stilled on the outside and inside as he closed the distance between them. He reached up, ran the back of his hand down the side of her face. She felt a spark when he did that, and her breath caught. A song, slower, with a steady, longing rhythm began. The singer asked the listener if she remembered a time they first met, implored her to come away with him. He called her his love, told her he wanted to tell her how much he loved her. Isabel knew the song. She loved it, had from the first time she'd heard it. She and this stranger looked at one another as it played until he looked away from her, at couples that had come together to dance to the song. When he looked back, he raised his hand in offering. She took it without breaking eye contact, without thinking.

He said nothing more but he saw her, saw what everyone else at that party had not seen. He didn't pull her back inside, where others were dancing, instead pulled her directly to the warmth of his chest, taking her away from every sound other than the song, everything else until there was only the two of them together. He brought her arm around his neck, like she'd done it all her life, and encircled her back with his other arm. His touch was slight as he laced his fingers with hers, his movements slow as he guided her body with his own. They moved barely in a half-circle as they let the song take them to a place where all they knew was one another. He bowed his head, closed his eyes, touched his forehead to hers. She turned her face so she could feel his cheek with her own. Neither made a move to kiss the other, but it was on Isabel's mind. She wanted to, wanted him to initiate that, but didn't at the same time. Somehow, hovering on the edge of that fire was more pleasant, more exciting, than falling into it.

They didn't break apart when the song ended. Isabel didn't realize when Thomas called from inside, but this man before her did. He was the one who stopped moving, brought his face back, looked into her eyes, barely an inch from hers. She could see a longing, a sadness now that had not been there moments before, and he tore himself away, piece by piece, backing away until he finally turned to look inside, answer Thomas's call from inside the apartment. Isabel stayed where she was, her hand still in his. Only when he took a final step back inside did he let go of her.

Lovely electricity, she thought as her eyes clouded, her throat tightened, as he moved from her sight now, leaving only a memory that she knew, for some reason, would last a long time.

She stayed there, dwelling in the moment until she heard Thomas call her name as well, and she snapped to. She took a breath, albeit ragged, and blinked a few times to get herself together and back into the current moment. Her cheeks were still hot and flushed when she walked back into the room. A lot of people had filed out, and she wondered just how long she'd lingered out there on that balcony. Thomas sat in a big, cushioned chair, tinkering with an acoustic guitar.

"Hey," he said when she emerged. There were a few people seated around, watching him, but now their eyes all turned to her. She couldn't look at them. She kept her eyes on Thomas.

"Hey," she answered and tucked her long dark hair behind her ears. Finished with the guitar, he held it out for her to take. She stood where she was, didn't move.

"What?" she asked. Her heart started up again.

He nodded once in her direction.

"Play that song you played for me at the studio."

Everyone still stared at her.

"Right now?"

"No better time." Now, of all times, he smiled.

She swallowed hard as she reached out to take the guitar and tried to smile. Well, at least she'd never have to see these people again. She was still halfway dreaming about her encounter with the man on the balcony when she sat opposite Thomas and adjusted the chords to her liking.

"Hey, Spence!" Thomas called into the kitchen, then turned back to Isabel. "You may as well meet all of your future band mates right now."

Spencer appeared in the doorway, stopped short, looked at Isabel with his warm blue eyes. He didn't move. Neither did she.

It was he who finally came forward, extended his hand.

"Isabel." His voice was nearly a whisper. For the second time that night, she took his hand. "Nice to meet you," he said, the half-smile returning.

"Uh, you too."

Dork, she scolded herself.

"Plays guitar and piano, sings, composes, and mixes songs," Thomas said. "And this is Greg, our drummer."

The short-haired, heavyset guy on the couch reached forward to shake her hand.

The tall blonde sitting to Greg's left smiled, half-waved in greeting. "And I'm Renee, Greg's better half."

"Costume mistress. And the best backup singer you'll hear anywhere." Greg winked at her and she half-slapped his arm.

Isabel smiled at them. She already liked them, could see the genuine love they felt for each other.

Renee turned back to Isabel. "I design a few sets," she admitted. "And help with images when needed."

"And sing," Greg reiterated.

"And sing," she conceded, rolling her eyes. She studied Isabel for a second. "I like your look a lot. I don't think you'll need any help once we start touring."

Isabel felt a rush when she said that, and couldn't quite imagine herself in front of a few hundred people, singing. She looked down at herself, her long black sweater-jacket over jeans and boots. Her dark hair was long, almost to the small of her back, her crescent moon necklace and long earrings silver. Her makeup was minimal, her skin pale as it always had been.

"Thanks," she said, feeling the blush rise in her cheeks again. She blinked, looked at the guitar. She'd forgotten how to play. Spencer came around the blue couch, but instead of sitting on it, he sat on the floor, bent his legs, placed his elbows on his knees, inches away from Isabel. He never took his eyes off of her.

Isabel turned back to her guitar.

Focus. She breathed in deeply, began strumming, singing the song she had sung for Thomas only a few hours ago. She felt she was off key, and too fast, rushing the song in the chorus, and couldn't quite lose herself in it the way she knew she needed to. She was too aware, too in the moment with these strangers all around. She knew this would be the final straw, that Thomas would tell her not to call them, they'd call her, blah, blah, blah. But, when she strummed that last chord, it wasn't Thomas's voice she heard. It was applause from everyone around.

"That was awesome," Thomas said, and Greg and Renee agreed. She looked at him, then over at them, expecting it to be some kind of joke, but they just continued praising, now talking amongst themselves rather than to her. She only looked away when she felt a soft stroking along her ankle, and turned to where Spencer was sitting.

He'd placed his hand on her leg, just once. "Beautiful. Isabel."

It wasn't clear whether he was talking about her or the song, and it took her a moment of looking into those eyes of his before she said, "Thank you."

He removed his hand from her slowly, just a second before Thomas's eyes landed on the two of them, but she still felt him, felt his hand on her.

"Well, Isabel," Thomas said. "I think it's safe to say you've got the job. But there is one condition—"

Isabel raised her eyebrows, waiting. Spencer got up, went into the kitchen. Even though her attention should have been on Thomas and his impending question, she couldn't help but watch as Spencer took a tumbler from one of the cabinets and poured just a bit of Jack Daniels into it.

He downed it just as Thomas said, "I'd like for you to go out with me."

"Aw," said Renee.

Spencer coughed uncontrollably on his whiskey. Isabel felt a slight catch in her chest. What? Had Thomas actually just said that? Spencer recovered and set the tumbler down, turned around, leaned against the counter, rested his hands behind him. Isabel's eyes darted from him to Renee to Greg to Thomas and then back again.

Thomas had just offered her a job. And he'd asked her out. In front of three other people. What—what the hell?

She swallowed hard and blinked several times. He was waiting. Everyone was. She couldn't drag this out any longer. *Oh, dear.*

Finally, she forced what she hoped was a convincing smile and said the only thing she could say, "Okay, yeah," and all the while thinking, *What have I done? And what am I doing?*

♫♫♫

Spencer turned the collar up on his jacket and pushed his hands deep into his pockets as he navigated the abandoned streets of the town square a little after two that morning. The little lights on the crepe myrtles lining the streets glowed like they did every night, but the light was soft, soft enough to allow nighttime dangers to hide in the shadows and jump out at the unsuspecting. Isabel was about a block ahead, sweater buttoned tightly around her, messenger bag crossed over her body. Spencer stayed close inward to the brick faces of the little shops and restaurants they passed so she wouldn't see him. She hadn't turned around once the whole walk home, but there she was: small and alone in the middle of the night and when she'd said her whispery good-byes to everyone minutes earlier, he decided he couldn't let her go all alone like this. He'd given her a head start so Thomas, his thief friend, wouldn't get the wrong idea—or maybe the right idea? Spencer shook his head now. Didn't make a difference, really.

The second he'd seen her, quietly navigating her way through groups of people she didn't know in a place she'd never been, he'd felt a pull. He didn't know how else to describe it. It was like desire took second place to the need he felt to follow her out to the balcony. He wasn't used to that feeling. Usually, women made it easy, walked up to him at parties, reached for him onstage. But then they wouldn't let go.

Was this how it felt, being on the other side, being drawn to someone without rhyme or reason? He felt like Odysseus without the ropes, going to the siren who, it was clear by her first question and startled look, didn't know she was one.

Strangely enough, that was what had made him want her more, reach out, pull her to him. He wasn't an idiot who believed in love at first sight, but he knew a mutual connection when he felt it.

She was different from the other women he usually went for, women he'd let catch him for a week or two. There was a sweetness in her, a quiet cry for protection. A good foot taller than her, he could do that, encircle her like a lion, and he wanted to.

He wanted to take her home, keep her safe. And that was something he'd never felt.

There a quietness even in her singing. Her voice was warm, velvet, but with an ironic edge. It calmed him as he sat there listening to her. He nearly joined in, only as a hum during her solo that evening, feeling that call again, but stopped himself just in time. This was her moment, not his, even if she didn't want it, which, he could tell, she didn't. Her shyness came through even when she sang. The way she looked down, at her guitar or her hands playing it, it was obvious she didn't know how good she was.

And when it was over, he had to reach out, feel something tangible.

But she would, in time, know how good she was. They would write together, sing together. He already knew it, knew how well their voices would harmonize.

Spencer stopped, watched as she unlocked a narrow door between a coffee shop and a gift boutique and went in, finally safe. He moved closer in to the silent street, leaned against a lamppost, and watched as a light came on in the second story of the building she'd entered. He would help her, be with her in this way, the only way that he could right now.

It was so cold he could see his breath coming out as smoke, and he felt it all the way inside and shuddered before turning and beginning his walk back to the little house he was renting during their stay in Laurel Springs.

It was almost three by the time he got there, but as he closed the door behind him, he turned on the lights, then the stereo, then the television. But nothing let him escape his siren, not the light, not Stevie Nicks commanding Tom Petty to stop dragging her heart around, not Gary Cooper waiting on high noon with Ian MacDonald. No. Isabel overpowered all of that.

He pulled out his phone, seeking a larger distraction since sleep was too much to hope for at the moment, saw he had two missed calls, a text and a voicemail. Looking at the numbers, he saw two of the missed calls were from Rachel, a girl he'd stopped seeing almost three months earlier, and one was from Anna, his latest dalliance that had lasted only a week. Rachel had left a message saying she was just calling to see how he was doing—just like she did every week—and Anna had sent a text. *"Busy tonight? Want to hang out later?"*

Spencer sighed and replaced his phone in his coat pocket. Their sweet voices, once sexy and alluring, were now laced with a pleading edge as they asked what he was doing that evening or weekend and waiting, always waiting, for him to ask them out just one more time.

Spencer leaned against the far wall of his living room and looked out at the night sky. Maybe this was a good thing, Thomas getting to Isabel before he did. This way, they could both remember tonight and he couldn't hurt her the way he had Anna and Rachel and other women. He always had the sad foresight of doing that when he met a woman he liked, and he met them often. But there was no premonition now. There was no smoke, either, as he sighed.

But he still felt cold.

He turned to look at the television again but his eyes landed on an open notebook on the coffee table, a notebook he kept ideas for songs in. It only took a minute of simply looking at it before he shrugged out of his jacket and went over to it, and picked up a pen.

♫ ♫ ♫

Thomas flipped the switch on the dishwasher before taking a last look around his apartment. Greg and Renee had stayed late to help him clean up the mess from the party and they'd taken care of most of it. Spencer, of course, couldn't be bothered to help out. He'd left with barely a good-bye right after Isabel had said her farewells and walked out.

The rest of the mess could wait until morning, Thomas decided, shedding his shirt and dropping it to the floor before collapsing into his bed. He closed his eyes but couldn't fall asleep right away. His mind was still reeling from the noise of the party and seeing Isabel again. She was cute, no doubt about it, he thought as he opened his eyes in the darkness. He turned his head to look out the window. A full moon glowed overhead in the sky. The girl could play, too, and could sing. She was going to add something to their band. He knew it. Despite that, though, he hadn't thought to make a move on her until tonight. He'd watched her as she surveyed the room, the groups of people talking, before finally walking out to the balcony. And he'd watched, too, as Spencer followed her out there. The guy had been talking to Rick, an artist that lived on the first floor of his building, but when Isabel sauntered through the room carrying that beer, Spencer just turned and went toward her like she was his for the taking, like he did with just about every woman he saw. And he didn't always have to go after them, either— hell, he rarely did. They always clamored all over him. Blue eyes, long hair, plus a hell of a guitar player and singer and ba-da-bing, here was heartthrob central.

Thomas punched his pillow and turned over. He'd watched the door to the balcony, though he didn't go out there once. He knew how long they spent out there, and it was a long time, just the two of them. He knew something was going on. And then that little creepy touch he gave her after she finished playing her song for everyone? What the hell was that?

That was the last straw, Thomas had decided. He was the one who'd found Isabel, not Spencer. And he was going to be damned if Spencer got one more thing of his. Thomas was the one raised in a musical family, the one groomed and trained in singing and practically every musical instrument one could play, not Spencer! Spencer's

parents hadn't even wanted him for crying out loud—
they'd abandoned him to his uncle when he was a kid.
And yet, here he was, the star, the natural talent that everyone flocked to, gave credit to! Where would he be if
Thomas hadn't asked him to join his band in high school?
Nowhere! Still training horses on his uncle's ranch, that's
where, and playing guitar on his back porch at the end of
the day, where he should be!

Thomas closed his eyes. He'd thought about firing
the dude several times, had wanted to and come close,
even. But then he'd look at the reviews of their album,
see the praising words critics gave to Spencer's songs,
see men as well as women singing along with his songs at
concerts, more so than they did Thomas's. And he knew.
Spencer had him tied. If he let Spencer go, all that would
happen is that Spencer would go off and make a huge solo career for himself. The band needed Spencer, not the
other way around.

But Thomas would be damned if Spencer got the
girl, too, on top of Thomas's career and band. He saw the
way Spencer looked at her. There was a light in his eye,
different from the way he looked at the many other wom-
en he'd take to on the road. There was a connection.

Thomas half-smiled as relaxation and sleep started to
sink in, little by little. The opportunity to ask Isabel out
was priceless, laid before him like a gift, and all he had to
do was open it. Her initial look had stung but Spencer's
coughing and gagging on his all-important whiskey had

more than made up for it. The sound of that was better than any song he'd written. And she'd accepted. Oh, he'd make her like him, all right, fall for him. He'd see to it. And she wasn't going to fall for Spencer. She was his. Finally, something was his, and there was nothing his dear friend Spencer could do about it.

Just then, his phone lit up with a new incoming call. He picked it up, stared for a couple of more rings before answering.

"Jessie?" he said into the phone.

Chapter 4

Three days after Thomas left a message on her voicemail, Isabel still hadn't called him back. She supposed that just about anyone would've been shy to see someone they hadn't seen in six years. It didn't help that Isabel had yet to forgive Thomas, that he had yet to ask for forgiveness because, in his mind, why should he?

He'd sent her a CD, the first recording she'd done with the band, though she already had her own copies, even had them downloaded to her phone. She supposed he was trying to entice her back, remind her of the good times. She listened to it while she took long walks in gray mornings on the road running alongside the beach, all the way to the pier, and to the end of it. She watched seagulls and dolphins in the distance and smelled the salty sea air as she listened to Thomas and Spencer's voices. She skipped over the ones that she'd done. She hated listening to herself sing.

Even today she found herself picking apart her own voice. She'd rushed a chorus there, she was off key here. Was she even in the right tempo?

Isabel sighed, leaning against the splintered railing, watching the ocean below dip and rise, so deep, so wide. It was perfect. It looked like it encompassed the whole world from this point. Her phone buzzed on the railing before her and she looked, took her ear buds out. She rubbed her forehead with the heel of her hand. She knew the number this time.

And she knew she may as well answer because he was just going to keep calling until she did. She had an answer, anyway.

It had changed about five times over the past few days but now she knew what she was going to say and do. She'd always known.

"Thomas," she said by way of hello when she brought it to her ear.

♫♫♫

Spencer sat at the end of the long laminated bar, going over the books and drinking coffee. The late afternoon sun shone in over the heads of the few patrons sipping their afternoon fixes, reading the paper, watching football on the TV in the corner. Scott stood at the other end, drying mugs and talking to Fred, who was eighty if he was a day, but who came in every day at four and stayed until nearly nine every night.

He barely drank more than a couple of cups of coffee, but it was obvious this was his place away from home. He was currently telling Scott something about the war in Korea, pointing his finger at the boy like he was personally responsible.

When the phone rang, Scott practically dashed over to it. Spencer half-laughed to himself as he turned back to the books.

"Spence!" Scott called. He looked up and Scott held up the phone.

Spencer took off his glasses—he couldn't read a thing without them nowadays—and walked around the bar, thanking Scott as he took the phone.

"Hello?" he said into the receiver.

"You ever answer your cell phone?"

It was Thomas. Spencer had seen where he'd called about five times since that first morning, wanting an answer about this reunion, his messages getting increasingly agitated.

"Occasionally," Spencer responded. "Guess you need an answer."

"Yesterday," Thomas said.

Spencer laughed. Already Thomas was resuming his boss position.

"Well, it was quite a thing you asked me," Spencer said. "I needed some time to think about it."

"Yeah, you and Isabel," Thomas said. "Look, I've already heard back from her. Are you in or not?"

Spencer halted when he heard Isabel's name.

"She coming back?" he asked.

Thomas was quiet for a long time. Then it was his turn to laugh. "Yeah, you'd like that, wouldn't you?"

Spencer wouldn't lie. He'd definitely like that, like to finish the unfinished business between them. But he wasn't responding to sarcasm. And it was clear that was all Thomas was going to give him.

Thomas sighed, as if he'd had enough of everything in life and was finding it hard to live on. There was a crack in his voice as he said, "Are you coming or not?"

His tone was a little more cordial, less hostile.

Spencer looked toward the sun in the windows as someone came in, the door slamming behind them, the answer to Thomas's question already formed in his mind.

Chapter 5

September 2009:

The next morning, Isabel awoke to the sun streaming in delicately under her blinds. The air was only slightly cold that morning, promising a warmer day. She turned over in her bed, letting consciousness come to her gradually as she basked in the dreams she'd had most of the night of Spencer. They'd consisted of hardly more than the memory of them together on that balcony in the night, just before the rain, but it was still nice to wake up to the thought of him.

"Spencer," she said, her eyes still closed. She liked the feel and sound of his name as she said it aloud. He hadn't said another word to her the rest of the previous evening, though they'd all stayed at Thomas's until nearly two in the morning. She hadn't said anything else to him, either. After Thomas had dropped the bomb of asking her out, any other exchanges with Spencer seemed...inappropriate.

But their eyes had met and lingered on more than one occasion, and every time they did, Isabel felt that same rush of electricity. She would've been content to simply look at Spencer and his eyes all night and all day, but deep down wanted something more in those lingering moments. There was something in those eyes, those looks, his voice, in the few words he'd said to her, that made her want to go near him, be next to him, talk to him.

She opened her eyes, surveyed the clothes she'd just shed to the hardwood floor last night before crawling into bed. There was another pile across the way. She stared, without really seeing it, before turning and taking a pen and one of many slender notebooks off of her nightstand. She flipped through it until she found a blank page and began writing.

The words, filled with images of dancing in the rain at midnight, close without the need to speak, being so near the edge of possibility, came fast and easy. When she was finished, she closed her notebook, didn't read over them. That would be for another time, another day. She sat back in her bed, peeked out the window, wondered if she could get away with pitching that song to Thomas. Would he catch on to what it was about? She thought about that as she stared out the window, watching the sunlight brighten the town square below her as a cloud moved, but never really answered the question in her mind.

It didn't matter, anyway. She'd still have it, even if she decided not to share it with the band and the rest of the world. Still halfway smiling to herself, Isabel got out of bed and walked around the Chinese screen she'd set up to separate her "bedroom," which consisted of nothing more than her bed, her oak dresser and nightstand, from the rest of the loft area. She walked through her little living area to her kitchenette to make coffee and saw that, despite the fact that she hadn't gotten in until almost three the night before, it was only a little after nine now. She'd never needed much sleep, and always did her best writing the less sleep she got, so maybe, just maybe, what she'd just written wasn't half bad.

Waiting as the coffee pot spewed and hissed before her, still halfway lost in her reverie, she thought about something Thomas had said to her the night before about Spencer, how he wrote and sang songs for the band, among other things. Thomas had played and sung a couple of songs for her at the studio the day before so she could hear them, make sure her style was the right fit. But she hadn't heard Spencer sing, hadn't heard the words he'd written. In fact, other than the few words they'd exchanged the night before, she hadn't heard him speak.

She looked at the clock. Nine-fifteen. Her favorite music store opened at ten. She stared at the clock a second longer before fixing herself a cup of coffee and—after several sips, a shower, and change, and much pacing and consideration—she tossed her notebooks in her messenger bag, threw it over her shoulder, and left her apartment. And at five minutes to ten, when sixty-year-old Ed Tyler got out of his creaky truck that was about as cantankerous as a rhino that had been shot in the behind, he half-limped on arthritis-plagued legs to the front of the music store he'd kept in business for more than thirty years and found Isabel out there waiting.

"Mr. Tyler." Isabel smiled and waved to her former boss. She reached out to help him with a large canvas bag he was carrying, but he waved her off.

"Ah, I've got it. How're you doing, there, Izzie?" he bellowed, giving her a half-hug when he approached. He smiled behind his thick glasses. "Hadn't seen you in a while."

He unlocked the door and flipped on the lights, illuminating the high-ceilings and endless rows of CDs, DVDs, even some tapes and vinyl records near the back. Though he was mostly partial to classic rock, as was evidenced by the Eagles song that burst from the speakers when he turned on the radio up front, he carried just about anything by anyone in his store, and she knew he'd have what she was looking for.

Isabel took her time as she made her way up one aisle, then down the next. She knew she could've asked Mr. Tyler for help, and he even offered, but she declined, instead preferring to scan the rows of music and faces of musicians by herself, coming across what she was looking for naturally, or finding it all on her own, like a treasure. She found herself slowing when she approached the S section of the store, and slower even still when she got to the Sh's.

She reached forward, flipped over tags and albums for Sex Pistols, Simon & Garfunkel, Simple Minds, but it was only when she got to Smashing Pumpkins that she realized she was well past the Sh section. Grimacing, she flipped back a few notches and could only just feel the fluttery pang of worry in her stomach when there it was.

The first album by Shiloh Ridge. Thomas had told her yesterday that he'd named the band after a place close to where he'd grown up in Georgia. Her hands were shaky as she reached out, took the CD from the shelf. The cover was a black and white photo, of the four of them standing on a railroad track with their backs to the photographer, overlooking a drop of some kind, though to where, the picture didn't reveal. Isabel could pick them out immediately.

Greg was seated, arms before him. A girl, the one she'd replaced and didn't know the name of, was a pencil, standing with her hands laced behind a shock of short blonde hair.

Spencer stood with his hands in his pockets, one foot resting on the rails before him, his quiet confidence coming through even in this picture. And Thomas. Isabel felt a small drop as she looked at him, off to the side, hands on his hips like he was surveying something before him.

That was the man she was going out with that evening, the one who was going to call in a couple of hours to settle when and where.

She took the CD to the front counter, where Mr. Tyler had begun organizing some old records.

"Look at this," he said, holding up a Blondie record. "Original recording."

"Nice," she said, nodding. "Worth its weight in gold?"

"To me it is," he said, taking the CD she'd set upon the counter and glancing at the cover. "Ah, this is a good one, too. Local band, started close by."

"I know," Isabel smiled, pleased to hear him say that. He listened to every album that came his way in his store. He slid the CD toward her.

"Aren't you forgetting something?" she asked, holding up the ten she'd retrieved from her pocket.

He waved it away. "You know your money's no good."

"Oh, come on, Mr. Tyler."

"Nope," he reiterated, sliding the CD farther toward her.

She sighed, dropping her shoulders, but still unable

to resist the urge to smile. "You're too kind to me."

"Hey, in case you forgot, you spent half your pay right here when you worked here."

He was right. This place had become her refuge years ago, even before she was old enough to work. She never could play sports, could never hit the ball during softball, or kick it during soccer season. The same went for art. Her art teacher, a young Earth mother with brown hair down to her waist who always wore long skirts and long beads, had pulled her aside after the third week of class and gently suggested maybe she take another elective.

Then they started poetry in her English class, and that's when the spark happened, and Isabel found herself looking up more poems, going to the library and checking out thick books of poetry by W H Auden, Browning, Dylan Thomas, Shakespeare, Anne Sexton, Cummings, Frost, William Carlos Williams, among countless others. By the time she'd started hanging out at Mr. Tyler's store, buying CDs with her allowance, she'd been writing her own poems for a couple of years, and was finding all kinds of poetic elements in the songs she'd hear.

Then one day, she was looking at one of the secondhand acoustics on display and he said: "You play?"

Isabel had nearly dropped the guitar. She hadn't even known he was standing near. She immediately felt her face flush and replaced the instrument, shaking her head.

Mr. Tyler picked it up, examined it. "You know, I've always thought a guitar picked its person, like the wands did in *Harry Potter*. You remember that?" She nodded. He turned the guitar over again before looking at her with upturned eyes. "When's your birthday?"

"November tenth," she'd told him.

He handed the guitar back to her. "Happy Birthday."

It was early January.

"Oh, I can't—"

"You like it, I can tell. And from the looks of it, I think it likes you, too."

Isabel stood staring at it, only took it when he offered to take it back if she found she didn't like it. So, she took it home and wrote her first song that night—a pitiful little number about endless roads and rivers and everlasting love, but it was something, something that led to other songs, and other instruments, and a start she always credited to Mr. Tyler. She still couldn't read a note of music, but somehow she could play and could hear something in it that she couldn't with sports or art. It was a something that actually led to her getting a paying job doing what she loved, and though she wasn't making the money that some of her classmates were who'd gone on to become pharmacists or dentists or lawyers, she knew it was a different type of success.

And now she was with a band.

Isabel now replaced the ten in her pocket and took the bag with her new treasure.

"Thank you," she said, the memories of how much she owed this man still in her mind.

She couldn't even wait until she got to her little two-door red Civic to open the CD. She was tearing away the plastic cover before even opening the door. Before slipping the disc into the player, she pulled the insert from the case and, when she found the third song was written and performed by one Spencer Logan, she jumped ahead to it. Her heart was already thumping and she was biting away on her nails when she heard the steady, easy rhythm begin.

She knew his voice right away, would have even if she hadn't seen it was him singing. His voice was a glide, just above a whisper, a summer night when the stars seemed close enough to touch. And then the chorus—a storm started and encircled. Isabel closed her eyes as the baritone of his voice rose higher, jettisoned like a wild horse galloping against wind and rain, took on a raw power that became the storm it was so much like. It was like oxygen after a long, hard run.

And then when he brought it back down again, ending the song with the same raspy heat he began with, Isabel again felt the edge of the fire she'd felt the night before with him out there on that balcony.

She listened to it again, reading the words as he sang them this time, and this time hearing him, or the persona he created, talking to someone, a woman, telling the story of their relationship, too passionate and fiery to last. He told it all against the backdrop of a fierce hurricane, building when the woman's fiery love turned to equally passionate hate when he couldn't give her what she needed.

Isabel was surprised to feel tears on her face when it ended. She drove around town for a long time, listening to the rest of the songs, blushing when a woman's voice, the woman she was replacing, sounded in the background. She never did a solo, and most of her singing took place in the background of Thomas's songs.

Finally, around lunchtime, Isabel met one of the only living relatives she had, her cousin, Kat, for lunch at the sandwich café downtown. The downtown square consisted of an array of quaint, brick-faced shops, restaurants, offices, the cafe that Isabel played in each night, all surrounding a two-story stone-gray courthouse. The sidewalks were sprinkled here and there with benches and delicate crepe myrtle trees that were encircled by wrought-iron and that glowed with little Christmas lights in the evenings.

Isabel was still dwelling in the album as she entered the sandwich shop and made her way to the little two-seater table where Kat was already sipping on an iced tea, holding up a menu, glasses sitting on the edge of her nose. When she looked up and saw Isabel striding toward her, her eyes widened and her jaw dropped and she got up, waving like she hadn't seen Isabel in about ten years, and hugged her.

"Hey, there, darlin,' how are you? You look just beautiful!"

Isabel hugged her back, smiling, thinking she'd never get tired of Kat's ferocious hugs. It was Kat who had taken Isabel in when her parents were killed in a car accident.

Isabel had only been five at the time and Kat was not only her mother's cousin, but her best friend.

She'd seen Isabel through those days of sports and art, making her feel a little less bad about sucking at those things. "Well, I think it's because you just don't like it. But, at least you know now and can just move on to something else," she had said at the time.

"So, how'd that audition go yesterday?" she asked now when they were seated.

Her bracelets, two on each wrist, jangled musically together as she laced her fingers on the table in front of her. Her short dark hair had recently had a body wave and danced all around when a breeze lifted, and she wore a long blouse printed with red poppies over black slacks and silver shoes, and long chandelier earrings sprinkled with red stones to match. Her lips were done in the same red to match.

Isabel opened her menu in front of her, but didn't look at it just yet. She nodded as she took a sip of the sweet tea Kat had known to order for her and said, "I got it."

Kat winked at her. "I knew you didn't have to be

nervous. You going to get to play your own songs? What's the next step?"

Isabel told her everything they'd discussed the evening before, how they were going to meet in the studio the next day, about the songs she was going to bring in. Kat listened with her usual face, head a little down, serious upturned eyes.

"Do 'Winter Rain,'" Kat encouraged, slapping the table before her for emphasis. "You have to, that one is one of your best."

Isabel laughed. That had always been one of Kat's favorites. She knew what was coming next.

"Oh, but no, only if you want to," Kat said, reaching for her tea and taking a sip.

"No, I plan to submit it," Isabel said. *And maybe another I just started on.*

After the waiter came and Kat remarked on what a good-looking guy he was, that he should go out for modeling or something, making him blush in the process, they ordered turkey sandwiches. Isabel was still half-giggling at Kat as he left, remembering a time Kat had taken Isabel to Myrtle Beach when she was about eleven. The beach was one of Kat's favorite places in the world—she went there at least four times a year and always stayed a week or longer.

But on this trip, as they spread their towels and Kat took out one of her novels she was always carrying around, they saw two surfers emerging from the water.

It was an unfamiliar sight on this coast.

Kat pointed them out. "Come on, I'm going to get me a picture of that cute one," she said to Isabel, referring to the one with a tangled mess of dark hair flowing past his shoulders.

Before Isabel could think, Kat was sashaying toward them with her camera, the turquoise sarong tied at her waist wafting behind her, leaving Isabel with no choice but to follow.

She couldn't look at them as Kat went on about how they were just two young girls—Kat was fifty-one at the time—from Laurel Springs who'd never seen real live surfers before, and those two were just adorable, would they mind posing for a photo?

The cute one was hesitant, but the other was jazzed. "Come on, bro, let's do it!"

Kat had nudged Isabel between them, and today a picture of her between two surfers in wetsuits, holding surfboards stood on Kat's mantle, right in front of a picture of Kat grinning beside an Elvis impersonator.

"Bring us a couple of hot fudge sundaes when we're about half done," Kat called to the waiter. She leaned forward and said to Isabel, so no one else could hear, "If I could remember what sex was like, I'd say the sundaes here are better than that."

She sat back in her chair, crossed her legs, and took another sip of tea, leaving Isabel to giggle once again. She shook her head as she took her notebook out of her bag, opening it to what she'd written that morning and sliding it across the table to Kat.

"I'd love to know what you think," she said.

Still holding her tea, Kat replaced her glasses on her face and held up the notebook, reading.

"Hmm," Kat said, still reading, a half smile inching across her face. She looked at Isabel.

"This is good," she finally said, putting the notebook down. "Especially the part about the rain. The last line is a little iffy, but you'll get it to work. I think you should use this one, too."

"Yeah?" Isabel smiled. Kat was an avid reader who would read anything you put in front of her. Though she was partial to Debbie Macomber, Nicholas Sparks, and Stephen King, Isabel never missed an opportunity to let Kat read her own work.

Isabel was still smiling, looking down at her notebook when Kat said, "So, who is he?"

"Who?" Isabel's head shot up, and Kat belted out one of her lovely laughs.

Isabel smiled, admitting inside that she did want to talk about last night. Again she reached into her bag, pulling out the CD, the only picture she had of Spencer. She pointed him out as she handed the case to Kat. Kat studied it for a minute, turned it over in her hand.

"Well, he's got nice hair, and a nice body, it looks like, but you can't really tell much more than that. That's where you come in."

Isabel raised her eyebrows.

"Go ahead, tell me," Kat said after the waiter set their turkey sandwiches in front of them, and Isabel did. She told Kat everything about the way she met Spencer, how they danced on the balcony, how he touched her leg just briefly after she played her song, complimented her.

"Sounds like a connection," Kat said, taking a bite of her turkey sandwich. "Or a crush, since you don't know one another, yet."

Isabel nodded.

"But there's going to be plenty of time for that soon, and based on what you've told me, I'm thinking you're going to have a lot more songs to write."

Isabel took a bite of her own sandwich and looked out at the town square, at the people beginning to emerge from stores and offices, making their way to the sandwich shop or other various restaurants for lunch.

"Well," Isabel began. "Maybe, I don't know…"

Kat took a bite of her pickle spear, looked at Isabel as she chewed.

Isabel finished the end of her story, told her all about how Thomas had asked her out.

Kat stopped chewing and dropped her sandwich. "He said *what*?" she asked.

"He was joking." *I think.* "Surely he wouldn't have said I didn't get the job if I wouldn't go out with him, right?"

"Still, what in the world could you have said other

than 'yes'?" Kat shook her head with exasperation as she took a napkin and wiped her fingers. "Putting you on the spot like that. I'm not sure I like him."

Isabel suddenly felt bad. Thomas really had seemed like he was joking, but even if he really did like her—she could feel her shoulders drop.

"What's wrong?"

Isabel looked up.

"You stopped eating, got that faraway look you do when you're writing," Kat continued.

"I don't know," Isabel admitted. "I mean, I guess I feel bad for not liking him in that way. For thinking so much about his friend."

"You met this Spencer guy first, right?"

"Well, I met Thomas first, but he didn't ask me out until after Spencer and I—"

"Right," Kat said. "So there wasn't a connection with you and Thomas? No flirtations or promises or vows or anything, right?"

"Right."

"Then you don't have a thing to feel guilty about." Kat looked out over the street as a car passed and took a sip of her tea.

Isabel had to laugh, even though Kat didn't, even though she, Isabel, felt exactly the same. Not sure what else to do, she plunged into the sundae the waiter had set before her.

"Love or your career," Kat said, licking the chocolate off of her spoon. "What a choice."

Isabel smirked. "Well, I wouldn't call it love…" *Just yet, anyway.*

Kat pursed her lips together and half-smiled. "But you do *like* Spencer."

Isabel couldn't look up. She nodded.

"And from what you've told me, he likes you, too. He's the one who made the initial contact and then did again after you played your song."

Isabel put her spoon on the half-eaten sundae, pushed it forward a little on the table so she could fold her arms over one another. She watched as a blue SUV inched past outside.

Kat sat back in her chair. "I have to say, I haven't really seen you like this before."

Isabel looked at her for clarification.

"Well, except when you've got writer's block."

Isabel raised her eyebrows and nodded. She had to admit, she was feeling a little like that, like she'd started something she knew was good, but had no idea where to take it now. A little lost and looking for a sign, any sign.

"But what I meant was, I've never seen you so immediately smitten."

Kat made a grand gesture with her left hand to elaborate. Isabel brought her hand up so she could rest her chin on her palm and scanned the street across the way, just in time to see Jerry McDonald enter the restaurant and walk up to the counter. He didn't see her right away as he placed an order and paid the girl up front. She flushed all of a sudden and tried to look away, but as the girl gave him the bag with his sandwich and chips, his eyes met hers a second too soon. Still red in the face, she tried to smile, raise her hand a little. He looked at her a second longer, but didn't smile or wave, just turned and walked out to his truck, opened the door to it, got in, and revved it.

Isabel rubbed her eyes. "Ironic," she said.

"What?" Kat asked.

Isabel pointed in the direction of Jerry's now departing truck. "That was Jerry McDonald who just came in."

Kat turned in the direction Isabel pointed, even though he was long gone. "Oh my," Kat said.

Isabel nodded, her hand over her eyes. One night about two months ago, after she finished playing a song in the coffee shop, Jerry, who she'd never met before, walked right up on stage and gave her a rose and told her he would like to buy her a cup of coffee. Amid the sound of "aw" from various people in the crowd, Isabel had said of course he could. They sat for two hours talking, though she couldn't get a word in edge-wise. Jerry's hands shook as he talked.

He'd kept drumming his leg and interrupted her just about every time she tried to talk to him. That had irritated her, but she agreed to see him again, giving him the benefit of nervousness after having approached her in front of everyone. If anything, though, their second meeting had been worse than the first. He'd taken her to a movie, some horror flick about a man with a hook for a hand. Not that she would've seen much in the way of plot without a distraction, but his commentary throughout hadn't stopped.

Then he'd started running his finger down her arm, much like the man with the hook, she'd supposed, and actually started feeding her popcorn from the bucket. He'd smiled and nuzzled her ear when she awkwardly took it, then he sat with a false pout with his chin perched on his fist waiting, she'd realized, for her to feed him popcorn. Which she just couldn't do.

That's when she'd gotten up. "I'm sorry. I'm really sorry. I have to go."

He'd followed her out to the parking lot, asking her what was the matter while she dug in her purse for her keys.

"I—" she'd began, pushing around her wallet, phone, lip gloss, searching for her blasted keys, which seemed to have disappeared. "I don't feel all that good. I think I'd better go home."

It wasn't a total lie. The thought of him feeding her and demanding the same from her had left her a little nauseous.

He hadn't put up much of a fight, but had kissed her cheek and told her to feel better, that he'd call her later. She hadn't been able to bring herself to answer his call for two days and when she finally did, he said, without so much as a hello: "Well, I was beginning to worry! I called the hospital *and* the police station!"

"Jerry," she'd finally cut him off. "We need to talk."

He hung up on her after she started to tell him that maybe they weren't that right for each other in the romantic sense, but that she'd still like to be his friend.

Isabel sighed now, reliving the entire memory of their short time together. Kat was right. Jerry hadn't been the first guy that she hadn't felt a connection with, a guy unwilling to give up until she spelled it out for him. She hoped that Thomas asking her out wasn't a sign of more of that to come.

"I still think you should've jammed a fistful of popcorn into that guy's mouth," Kat said, bringing her back. "He would've gotten the picture, then."

Isabel had to laugh. She shook her head and tucked a strand of hair behind her ear.

"But in all seriousness, hon," Kat continued. "Don't write off this connection with Spencer just because someone else asked you out before he did. Like I said, I've barely ever seen you take to a guy and now that it's happened, well, I think it might be worth exploring."

"What about Thomas?" Isabel asked. She dropped her chin into her palm again.

"Well, keep your promise of going out with him since you've already made it, of course. But—" Kat took a sip of her tea and stared into the distance for a few seconds. "Just don't make anymore that you're not sure you can keep. Get my drift?"

Isabel smiled. "Yeah."

She sat back and sighed. As for right now, for this writer's block type of feeling she was having, she knew what she needed to do, what might give her more clarity. She needed to read, to lose herself in the words of others for a while so that her own might come forth again. So, when she and Kat finished up their lunch, Isabel promised to call the next day, and, instead of making her way back to her apartment, she crossed the street to George Carter's bookstore where she'd lose herself in the dim lighting, the classical music he always played, the smell of coffee and oak wood countertops and shelves.

"Hey, Isabel," George said, barely looking up from a large notebook as she pushed open the heavy glass door.

"Hey," she returned.

The bookstore was one of her frequent hangouts, too. She made her way to the poetry section in the back of the store, picked up a couple of anthologies, and had just turned to go sit in one of the deep, comfy armchairs when the little bell that sounded every time someone opened the door rang again. Isabel looked up and there he was, tall and broad, long hair as wild and disheveled as it had been the evening before.

He didn't see her, but Isabel's heart and stomach jumped, and she took a step back, dropping one of the books. She scrambled to pick it up and, when she looked up again, he was gone, just like a ghost or a reverie that just disappeared.

Isabel felt her shoulders drop as she looked all around. She turned to make her way to the front of the store again and set her books and her bag on a chair near the front window where the sun was shining in warmly. When she looked up, she saw him standing just where she'd been seconds before, in the poetry section. He was as still as a statue, reading something from a thick hardback. She could feel the same warmth in her stomach rising to her chest and smiled without being able to help it, almost without even realizing she was doing it.

'*Don't write off this connection,*' she heard Kat's voice say again.

Isabel took a breath, trying to steady herself, and blinked a few times. She couldn't bring herself to approach him. She was too afraid. So, she did what she hoped was the right thing. She took one of the books she'd set on the chair, turned so the sun would capture the amber in her hair, opened the book, and began reading.

See me, she prayed. *Talk to me. I want to talk to you.*

She leaned against the chair, kept her eyes on the book before her. She could hear footsteps, the sound of the bell clanging now and then. Finally, her knees began to ache and she had to sit down. She dared to look up but didn't see Spencer, not even in the poetry section again. She grimaced.

Had he left and she just didn't see? She sighed, feeling as if she'd betrayed herself somehow, and turned to look out the window just as the sun moved behind a white cloud in the distance, just as she heard a voice say, "Wild honey."

She turned, startled. Spencer stood a few feet away, on the other side of a chair. She couldn't help but smile. "What?"

"Your hair," he said, gesturing. "The way the sun shines on it, it's—it's the color of wild honey."

She looked at him a moment. No one had ever said anything like that to her before. She liked it. "Thank you."

He stayed where he was. So did she, and she thought about the song she'd heard him sing on the CD earlier today, could now picture him singing it on stage, strumming his guitar, maybe turning once or twice to look her way as she sang backup.

"Do you dance?" he asked.

Isabel shook her head to bring herself back from her daydream. *You mean like we did last night?* She couldn't help thinking. That was the first question that came to her mind.

"Off the wall question, I know," he said. "It's just…well, my mom was a dancer with a company in Atlanta and I've just seen a lot of dancers. Your posture, your small shoulders—they're just like a dancer's."

Isabel looked down at her shoulders and arms then back at him. "Thanks. I don't dance, but thanks."

He continued to smile, but turned, as if he were about to leave. Isabel panicked and blurted out, "Unless you count the shag."

He raised his eyebrows. She could feel her face turn three shades of red.

"The dance, I mean," she said, half giggling, shaking her head, closing her eyes. When she opened her eyes again, he was still smiling.

"I knew what you meant," he said.

Isabel sighed, feeling a little more relaxed now, a little bolder. "Do you want to sit?"

Spencer looked at the chair before him, came around, sat across from her. "So, you dance the shag. Kind of a beach dance, isn't it?" he asked, settling into the chair.

Isabel nodded, told him about Kat taking her in after her parents died, how they went to the beach all the time, and how Kat had taught her to dance that dance right there on the dunes with the ocean crashing behind. At first, she thought she was saying too much, giving too much information to someone she hardly knew, but Spencer just sat, resting the side of his face on his hand, smiling during the appropriate parts in her story, nodding here and there.

"You're close with her, I can tell," he said when she was finished.

Isabel nodded, settled back into her chair.

"My uncle raised me, from the time I was around ten."

Isabel raised her eyebrows, hoping he'd continue with his story. He did.

"Yeah, my mom's brother. She was busy traveling with the company a lot. Didn't think that was the best way of life for a kid. Jack—that's my uncle—raises and trains Quarter horses and so, before I knew it, I was feeding and watering them, mucking out stalls, grooming and riding, too. But my favorite part was always the end of the day when we'd sit on the back porch after dinner and he'd play his guitar and sing these old country tunes I'd never heard of. He was the one who taught me to play."

"Hmm," Isabel said, smiling, picturing everything he was telling her. "He teach you the piano, too?"

Spencer shook his head. "Taught myself on some old baby grand that was my grandmother's. He keeps it in the den."

"Ah." Isabel nodded. Then something occurred to her. "Your father?"

He shrugged. "Don't know, really. He was a dancer, too. I know that much. Mom never talked that much about him, but when she did…well, it's pretty obvious that they had what you'd call a tumultuous relationship."

"You've never even seen him?"

"Oh, I saw him." Spencer nodded. "All of the other dancers at the company told me I looked exactly like him. I saw a few pictures of him and my mom dancing in some productions. I think those pictures still hang in the main hallway of the company."

Spencer's voice faded as he stared into space. He took his time with his next thought. Isabel liked that. He wouldn't speak until he found just the right words.

"They were the star dancers of some of the major productions of that company."

"You don't know what happened?"

Spencer shrugged. "Mom didn't really like it when I brought him up, and everyone else I asked at the company just told me he took off for some company in New York right after I was born."

"Hmm," Isabel said again. She ran her hand along the armrest of the chair. "Your mom still dance?"

Spencer curled his lips under for a moment before answering. "She's buried in Covington, Georgia."

A heaviness set deep inside Isabel's chest. "I'm so sorry."

He nodded in thanks. "Lung cancer. Like a lot of dancers, she liked to smoke."

Isabel suddenly felt ashamed and looked away. When she looked back, Spencer was looking out the window behind her.

"Hey, I was going to grab some coffee after I pay for these," he said, holding up his books. "You interested?"

Isabel smiled. He'd said just what she'd wanted to hear.

After they got their coffee, they took their time walking along the sidewalk of the town square. Most of the lunch crowd had thinned out and they pretty much had the place to themselves.

"So, how did you guys end up in this small town, looking for another bandmate?" she asked. *How did I get so fortunate that you found me?*

"Traveling," he said. "We play a lot of gigs at fairs and events, things like that, and Thomas insists on advertising in the smaller towns, said those are the places where the hidden jewels are. Didn't realize how right he was—"

Spencer didn't look at her and didn't finish as he sipped some of his coffee. Isabel took a sip of her coffee, too, knowing they had to let the moment pass by. Her date with Thomas demanded that. When she swallowed her coffee, she reached to change the subject.

"So, you read poetry?" she asked, pointing out his purchases in the bookstore. He'd bought two anthologies, one of poetry and one of short stories.

He looked at the bag before nodding and taking a sip of his coffee. "I do," he said. "Started when I found this ancient poetry book by...what was that man's name?...Alan someone. Anyway, I found it on my uncle's bookshelf. It obviously hadn't been touched in years because it and every other book on the shelf were covered in dust. Anyway, I read it and then found one by Frost, one by Yeats, Byron, an old Shakespeare reader, and well, I just didn't stop."

"Hmm," Isabel said, smiling and taking a sip. She

told him about how she discovered her love of it, too, when she was a teenager and awkward at just about everything else.

"It's good stuff," he agreed. "The way they make every word count. Drew me to look at songs differently and eventually write my own."

He nudged her with his shoulder as he said that last part and she turned to smile at him.

"Who's your favorite?" she asked.

"Poet?" he said. She nodded. He didn't have to think.

"Oh, that's easy. Auden. 'The More Loving One.'"

Isabel felt a small jolt in her chest. Auden was one of her favorites, too, and that was her favorite by him. She found herself stopping, bringing Spencer to a stop beside her. She thought about telling him that was the very poem that drew her to poetry, but thought he'd find it too unbelievable, just as she did. So, she just stood and smiled for the longest time, and though he raised his eyebrows in question, he eventually smiled back.

"Sorry, I—" she began, shaking her head. "I was just remembering that poem from school. It was good. Good stuff, like you said."

They talked a while longer about other poets they admired—Whitman, Yeats, Frost, and even some by Auden. They recited lines back and forth, finishing verses the other had started. But Isabel still never mentioned her connection to Auden's work, deciding to keep it inside, a small secret of sorts.

When they finished talking, another quiet moment passed, one in which Spencer might take her hand, or touch the side of her face, and they broke eye contact. Again, Isabel couldn't help noticing, there it was the warmth in her chest, the rapid beating of her heart as they were content to simply see each other, dwell as another moment presented itself. Another opportunity they'd have to just miss.

Spencer cleared his throat and pushed his hair back. "Yeah," he said. "Good stuff."

"You know, I picked up your first album this morning," Isabel said, trying lighten everything.

"You did?" Spencer asked, the blue flame in his eyes glowing a little brighter. "And? What's your verdict?"

He pointed at a bench where they had a seat just inches apart from each other. A little closer and Isabel could've taken his hand without thinking. Just a little closer.

"I loved it. The sound you guys have—it's exactly the type of band I was hoping to play for."

"We," he said, taking another sip of his coffee.

"Hmm?"

"Use first person. You're part of us, now."

Isabel grinned. "I liked your songs. Especially the one called 'Like a Hurricane.'"

Spencer laughed and dropped his head between his knees for a minute. When he came back up, she could see he'd turned red.

"What?" she asked, returning the laugh.

"Ah, nothing," he said, shrugging. "It's just...I'd written it so long ago. I can't believe Thomas wanted to use it in the first place."

"How old were you when you wrote it?"

Spencer squinted, looking in the distance at the row of stores across the way. "Fifteen or sixteen?" he mused.

"Wow."

Spencer looked at her and she realized she'd just said that word aloud.

"Surprised?" he asked, and took a sip of his coffee.

"No, it's not that," she said. "It's just—" *It's so mature, so lovely. The words you use, the ideas all apply to relationships, or the end of them, rather. I can't believe it was written by someone so young.* She took a breath, tried to communicate her thoughts without seeming insulting. "I just...it's such a mature piece, deep. You, you really communicated the dynamics of relationships well."

Isabel inwardly rolled her eyes at herself, feeling stupid for stumbling over her words. Writing was such an easier form of communication. She thought about the song she'd written about him, their time together, that very morning, how it rested in her bag this very moment.

"Thanks, Isabel," he said.

She knew his song was about a girl and was curious, but at the same time didn't want to know. She liked it like this, just the two of them, the way he looked at her, listened to her, the way he said her name. She could feel her back straighten, her shoulders drop when he said it. Suddenly, she was sad, and had to blink a few times and look in the opposite direction. She wondered if either of them were ever going to acknowledge the proverbial elephant in the room. She found herself wanting it to happen but at the same time not.

Spencer pulled his own messenger bag onto his lap, began rummaging until he found a tattered black and white notebook. He didn't say anything as he flipped over pages filled with scribbles and cross-outs until he got to a page near the end. He'd crossed nothing out on this one. At nearly a full page, it was a clean copy.

"Ah, here it is," he said. He looked at it a moment. "I couldn't go to sleep last night. The TV, the radio, none of it could distract me from my own thoughts, so I finally just decided to put them down. I don't know if I should show this to you." He was still looking at the notebook before him. "Especially since Thomas—" He shook his head. "Ah, what the hell," he said before offering it to her.

Isabel stopped breathing for a moment, took the notebook with shaky hands. At first, she couldn't see the words. Here was someone, a musician, an accomplished songwriter, showing her of all people, before anyone else in the world, his work. She rubbed her hand briefly over the page before focusing. His writing was scribbled, quick, slanted, like he was trying to stay with the words as they came forth in his mind.

Isabel read of images of night, of a woman, a siren, with long hair the color of wild honey flying behind her. She was quiet, alone, and small. She drew him to her without a word, without knowledge, then disappeared like the night giving way to day.

Isabel looked at his words for a long time. At first, she didn't—or didn't know how to, rather—respond. She swallowed hard, realizing that this was Spencer's acknowledgment of their moments last night. She curled her lips under and pressed them hard together, and had to laugh out loud. Otherwise, she might cry.

"That bad?" he asked with a smile.

"No, not at all, it's just —you wrote about me!" She was still laughing. No one had ever done that before. She wasn't used to having that type of effect on someone.

"Yeah, sorry. Like I said, I couldn't really sleep."

She looked at him and he just looked back with that half smile she was becoming dangerously fond of and then he said, almost as an afterthought, "Have you ever sung a duet?"

Isabel shook her head.

"Would you like to?" he asked. "On that one, with me? I know some of it would have to be re-worked so it would make sense as a duet, but after hearing your song and your writing style last night, I think it might work nicely with…"

"Yours," she finished in a quiet voice.

He nodded.

"Y—yeah I'd love to," she stumbled. She blinked several times and had to turn away again.

"Awesome," he said, his voice almost a whisper. He tore the sheet out of the notebook, gave it to her to keep. "If you want to play around with it, add your own stuff in, I'll do the same and talk to Thomas later about it."

Isabel took the paper, but, wouldn't he need it?

"Nah, had it committed to memory before I wrote it all down," he said when she asked as much.

Isabel folded the paper, put it in her bag, in the notebook where she kept her words about him, so it would be safe. She already had a feeling of what she would add. Somehow, she was just a bit happier when she tucked the paper in there. She sighed just before Spencer made a move to get up. He held out his hand to help her to her feet and she smiled, thanking him.

"You're welcome, Isabel." Again, the velvet summer night touched his voice.

It was cooler by that point in the day, but they walked slowly along the all but abandoned sidewalk.

"Thanks," Isabel said as they stopped in front of her building. "For this afternoon."

"Yeah," Spencer agreed. "It was fun."

"I'll look this over tonight," she promised, patting her bag.

He waved her off. "Whenever you get a chance."

They stood, just facing one another for a long time. It was almost like the awkward moment at the end of a date.

Then, for the second time in twenty-four hours, Spencer reached up to run a hand along her cheek. It was cold out, but his hand was warm, like a blanket in front of a fire. Isabel closed her eyes to his touch, letting herself feel the ember she'd felt the night before just one more time. When she opened her eyes again, he was still looking at her. He took a step forward, closing the distance between them just as her cell phone started chiming and vibrating in her pocket. She closed her eyes again.

"And with that," he said, removing his hand and pointing at the phone she pulled out, the one that was now displaying Thomas's number. "I'm going to leave."

"Oh," she said. *You don't have to.* She knew otherwise, though.

"It's okay," he said, backing up, smiling again. "I'll see you tomorrow at the studio. Thanks again for today."

Isabel watched as he walked away, fast, and hoped her voice didn't crack as she answered Thomas's call.

♫♫♫

That night, Thomas met her at a little Italian restaurant called Roman's.

"I look forward to seeing you," he half-whispered into the phone, and hung up before she had a chance to respond.

It was already dark when Isabel began making her

way to Roman's—she insisted on meeting him there rather than him picking her up—and many of the shops were closed, their windows emitting only the softest of lights. She'd never been there, except to get take out maybe once a month, but now she noticed what a romantic air the place had—the soft lighting, the red and white checkered tablecloths, the candles on each table placed in green incandescent wine bottles, tables strategically placed around a small dance floor in the middle of the restaurant.

Yes, she thought. It was clear this was a date in Thomas's eyes. It was this, coupled with his eager smile and wave from a booth near the back that now bothered her.

Isabel nodded once, made herself smile as she walked toward him.

"Thomas." She held out her hand in offering. He not only took it, but pulled her to him with a jerk so he could kiss her cheek. It was only when she jumped back that he laughed.

"Sorry, getting a little overzealous, I guess," he said and gestured for her to sit down across from him.

Isabel touched her face, feeling a little flushed as she did so.

"I have to tell you, I just couldn't wait to see you," he said as they settled into their seats.

"Oh?" Isabel asked, trying to smile again as she opened her menu. "Why?"

"Why?" he repeated. It was clear he thought she would be flattered by what he'd said.

Isabel cleared her throat, shook her head. "Sorry. Um, hey, I picked up your first album."

"Yeah?" He lit up again. "What did you think?"

A young waitress set two waters in front of them and told them the specials of scampi and vegetarian lasagna. Thomas waved her off just as Isabel was about to open her mouth to order the lasagna. He held up a finger to her, too.

"If you don't mind, I'd like to make a suggestion."

Isabel raised her eyebrows. How could he know what was good here? He was a visitor. Nonetheless, she held out her hands for him to go on.

"We'll both have Filet Mignon, medium rare, with a side of spaghetti."

Isabel raised her eyebrows again. She had to admit, that did sound good. The waitress took their menus and asked if they wanted anything other than water.

"Red Zinfandel," Thomas piped up again.

He didn't even ask if I drink, Isabel thought, clasping her hands together and resting the side of her face on them. What if she were an alcoholic? She almost immediately scolded herself as he looked back at her and smiled. He really had no idea, and if he liked her—she shook her head and closed her eyes before reaching for her water and taking a sip. That'd be a bridge she'd have to cross when she came to it.

"Damn," he said, watching her. "You really are beautiful."

Isabel's water went down the wrong way and she began coughing. Okay, maybe she was already at that bridge. Thomas laughed and touched her hand that was resting on the table. She fought the urge to pull it away, not wanting to hurt his feelings, but could feel it stiffen under his touch.

He was already wanting too much, was crossing her human contact circle a little too quickly. But he was also the one who brought her into her dream. She could focus on her music full time.

She didn't know if it was that or him that made her feel scared. She shook her head to gather focus and went to change the subject again.

"I love your album," she went on. "That's just the type of sound I play, the kind I've been looking to join."

Thomas took his hand from hers so he could gesture as he talked about starting the band back in high school, just him and Greg, how his dad and mom worked eight-to-five jobs during the day but played in a local band in Covington by night, mostly covers of The Eagles, Fleetwood Mac, Tom Petty, The Allman Brothers. Thomas would usually tag along to their rehearsals and shows, though he mostly remembered long-haired, long-moustached hippies in jeans and T-shirts, but, boy, could they play and sing.

He would almost always end up asleep on a big couch or chair backstage, a big pair of headphones over his ears to drown out the sound. "But, it wasn't all bad," he went on, telling her how that helped him discover his own sound.

He supposed he was destined to play music. From the moment he picked up that first guitar during a break at rehearsals, he saw that certain proud twinkle in his father's eye. He learned everything from every member—the guitar, the drums, keyboards, even learning how to record and produce an album, sitting there in that studio with tall, burly Mr. Stephenson, their producer, who taught him the controls and which buttons did what, how to make something or someone sound better from behind the scenes. His mother taught him to sing and how just standing there wasn't enough.

"'Roy Orbison could get away with it because he was just that good,'" Thomas remembered his mother telling him. "'But his was a once in a lifetime, one in a million voice, so he was about the only person who could. You need to have a presence, a look, *energy*.'" Thomas held his wine up, staring into space for a moment. "You know, I never could master that part of the act." Then he shrugged all of sudden, like it never really mattered. "But, that's okay because Spencer handles that just fine."

Isabel felt a small startle in her chest. She'd been so caught up in what Thomas was saying. "He's a performer?" she asked, taking her fork and pushing her remaining spaghetti around on her plate.

Thomas nodded, finishing his wine and setting it before him. "Look us up on YouTube," he encouraged. "There's a clip from a fair we played in Asheville last summer. Illustrates it pretty well."

Isabel nodded only once as she kept her eyes on her plate before her, but she knew as soon as she got home she'd be on her laptop, looking for that video.

"Women love him," Thomas continued. "And he loves them right back. I'm surprised he didn't make a move on you."

Isabel jumped, sending her fork flying off to the side before it bounced off the booth and clattered to the floor.

Thomas watched it all with raised eyebrows. "I'm just saying—" he began, taking his time, looking her square in the eye. "—that you're attractive."

Oh, stop that already, she thought, and ran her hands through her hair. "You mentioned that," she said, sitting up and taking a sip of her own wine.

"You not comfortable with me saying that?"

Don't lie. Don't make any more promises you can't keep. "Not really," she admitted.

Thomas sat back, eyebrows raised.

"Sorry, I don't mean to be rude."

"No, it's okay," he said, folding his arms across his chest. "It's just that you're perfectly honest. I like that."

Isabel felt her face break into a half smile at that

compliment. Still, she had to know something. "I'm sorry I flipped out there for a minute," she said. Thomas smiled. "It's just that…" Isabel struggled to say what she meant without Thomas picking up on her feelings for Spencer. "…it's just that Spencer didn't seem like that type of guy, the one you describe. He seems more quiet and reflective." *Like me.*

Thomas's voice took on an authoritative tone. He leaned forward and placed his fingertips on the table, all knowledgeable and serious now. "The thing about Spencer," he said, as if talking about a child he was dropping off at daycare for the first time. "Is that there are two sides to him. The one you saw last night—"

And today.

"And the one you haven't seen yet, the stage presence he brings. The one all the girls go after."

Isabel set her wineglass down, kept her fingertips on the stem. She wasn't entirely surprised. He was the son of two performers. It was in his blood. Still, though, two sides to him? She really had to see that video because she was having just a little bit of a hard time wrapping her head around it.

"And believe me when I tell you, he welcomes their attention *and* affection with open arms—no pun intended."

Isabel felt that shock again and took her hand off of her wineglass a second before she accidentally flung it across the table. When she recovered enough, she took it and downed what was left in it. This person Thomas was describing did not sound at all like the sweet, grave person she'd spent the afternoon with, the person she'd listened to and who'd listened to her, who wrote a song about her hours after meeting her, the person she saw much of herself in.

Isabel tried to seem nonchalant. "Well, I guess I'll just have to watch the video."

She turned her head just in time to see a few couples making their way to the dance floor. For a moment, she thought Thomas was going to ask her to dance. But, he just sat back, pressing his back against the wall just as she had, and watched them, too.

"What about you?" she asked, still watching the couples. She felt the need to change the subject. To be honest, she'd liked listening to Thomas when he was talking about starting the band. It felt like talking to an old friend she'd known for years. It was when he'd started all but badmouthing his friend to her that bothered her, and put a darkness over the evening. She felt she needed something to lift it.

"What about me?" he asked.

"Do the girls come after you?"

He looked at her.

"What would you do if they did?"

Isabel turned back and raised an eyebrow. Was he asking if she would be jealous?

He laughed. "No, not hardly. Though—there was someone."

Isabel turned back to the dance floor, annoyed again, and watched a middle-aged couple join together and begin dancing in a semi-circle, both gray and with glasses. The man was a good head taller than the woman. They moved close together, smiled as they looked at one another. They really seemed in love, Isabel observed, unburdened by outside forces.

"Her name was Jessie," Thomas continued. "She played bass for us for three years. Left six months ago."

Isabel turned head so she could look at him. He didn't continue. He just looked at the same couple she'd been watching. She'd seen that look Thomas was wearing, but it was on Jerry's face that she'd seen it when he'd come back to the coffee shop to hear her sing. It was a hurt look, a pain concealed. Isabel sighed, could see and feel warning lights going off in her head, but ignored them anyway.

In this moment, in his sadness, she liked Thomas. She felt for him the way she might an elderly person lying alone in a nursing home bed, or a child who'd fallen and skinned his knee. So, she did something she'd never done. She pushed herself out of the booth, stood up, and extended her hand.

"I like this song," she said. "You want to dance?"

Thomas didn't look at her until he'd risen from his side of the booth.

"I thought you'd never ask," he said, taking her hand.

Thomas wasn't as tall as Spencer, so Isabel was able to rest her chin on his shoulder as they danced through one song and then the next. It was nice, comfortable, but it wasn't fire or electricity she felt as she danced with this partner this evening. It probably never would be.

And she didn't know what troubled her more, that awareness or the way Thomas held her hand as he walked her home and brought it to his mouth just once before watching her unlock the door to her building and walk away from him.

Chapter 6

December 11, 2016:

A week after Thomas's call, Isabel was piloting her little red Civic along Highway 26, starting the two hundred-fifty mile trek back to her hometown. It didn't take long for her to pack up the little life she'd made for herself at the beach. She paid Mrs. Beatty, the kindly old woman who rented her the second floor of her two story home, for the remainder of the year, and the woman promised to keep an eye on the few things she'd left behind. The only trouble she had was from Winston, the owner of the coffee shop she'd been playing nights in, who told her he'd have a hell of a time finding someone to come in and play and sing for the evening coffee crowd.

She left behind the little life she'd been living for the past few years late that night, preferring to drive under the stars and by the light of the moon, with few cars around. The steady stream of Shiloh Ridge's CD in her player cycled through. She was hoping it would ready her and steady her somehow, but all it seemed to do was bring back memories that made her nervous. As usual, the more nervous she got, the quieter she got.

And so, just as the sun was steadily creeping over the quiet streets of Laurel Springs, Isabel navigated her way amongst the mill houses, shopping centers, drug stores and restaurants local only to the small town. She came into the town square, as unchanged as the day she left, and parked her car in the town parking lot, a stranger now without a home in her hometown. She was sad when she got out of her car and into the chill of the dawn air, and she buttoned her black pea coat.

Her legs and back were stiff from the five-hour drive and she had to stretch. She looked all around and saw that only the coffee shop, the one where she used to live above and play in every night, glowed from within, the only place open. She thought about going in for a cup of coffee, but decided against it. She didn't know if she would see anyone she knew, and she just wasn't quite ready, not yet.

Besides, Kat was expecting her in a couple of hours.

She'd have coffee there and bask in the quiet solitude Kat could give her before she had to revisit the people she'd avoided for so many years.

Isabel put her hands in her pockets as she wandered the streets, looking in darkened windows of stores that were not yet open. Had it really been "so many" years? She knew a lot could happen in that span of time, that people, children, especially, could come out on the other end of that time frame virtually unrecognizable. But had she? What had she done, really? When Spencer hadn't returned any of her calls or messages, she'd traveled the southeast, playing in bars and coffee shops. She never tried signing to any other label, though there were offers.

Even though she played new little songs she'd written in front of the small crowds every night, somehow otherwise falling off the radar, laying low, and just disappearing was comforting. It was like she could exist without remembering, without worrying. It was like reading a good book cover to cover or going to sleep and dreaming—everything becoming a different place and time for a while. But somehow, Thomas, or his manager, rather, had found her.

Isabel had just passed the coffee shop and was moving under the green awning of Hampton's clothing boutique, when she happened to look across the square to the other side where Carter's bookstore and Roman's still were.

That's when she saw him, running, dressed entirely

in black and moving so fast, she almost missed him. She backed up against the brick building, moving farther into the darkness, though he probably wouldn't have seen her, anyway. He was looking down, focused only on the sidewalk before him. Even from this distance, she knew it was him.

His body, his movements, his shaggy hair moving in the wind—they all gave Spencer away. He turned the corner and was gone, just like that, just as quickly as he'd appeared. He was probably running past her car now. If he even noticed it, he wouldn't know it was hers, just like he'd never know she'd seen him running in the dawn of a new day.

Isabel watched where he'd been for a long time. When she finally found enough of herself to push away from the wall, begin her walk again, she was only a little surprised to feel tears that had fallen down her face some time ago.

Chapter 7

D amn it," Isabel said the next morning, furiously erasing the words she'd written mere seconds ago.

She'd arrived at the studio early that day, pushed open the oak and bubble glass door. A small, round woman with long, dark curly hair and glasses had been glancing over a paper and coming down the stairs near the front when she looked up and said, "Oh, hi, you must be Isabel."

She came forward to shake hands and introduced herself as May Dorn, the owner of the studio. Isabel smiled, relaxing in the woman's pleasantries. She guessed May to be in her early fifties.

"Thomas said you'd be coming in today. Come in, have a look around. My husband, John, is out getting some bagels and said he'd be back soon."

She showed Isabel the downstairs lounge to the left. It was simple, with only a couple of couches and chairs, and coffee tables. A burgundy rug stretched almost the length of the room.

"It doubles as a consultation/waiting room," May explained. "Meeting room's across the way." She pointed to a wood-paneled room that had a stone fireplace and housed a long oak table surrounded by about a thousand chairs. "My office is in the back. Come on upstairs, I'll show you the studio and where you'll be doing most of your work here."

She led Isabel upstairs, showed her the little kitchenette where she assured her that coffee would always be available, then the upstairs lounge and writing room just beyond that that housed a roll top desk, a couch and a couple of armchairs with a coffee table between them.

"Bathroom's off to the side of this room," May explained. There was another stairwell all the way at the end.

"What's that?" Isabel asked, pointing.

"Oh, that leads to the roof," May said. "It pretty much stays unlocked so feel free to go on up anytime you feel like it. I have a lot of musicians who like to go up there to take breaks, get away from noise, scream if they feel their voice needs it. And here's the studio."

She pointed out an enormous room across the way that had miles of computer screens and keyboards at a long glass desk. A smaller isolation booth was walled off at the side and a large panel with about a million buttons covered the desk that stretched across the entire lower half of the far wall. A window above it overlooked another, larger isolation booth. That was Isabel's favorite room, she decided. It wasn't wood-paneled like the rest of the building.

Instead, it was painted a pale blue, was carpeted and high-ceilinged. A drum set was off to one side, keyboards to the other. Guitars and other instruments of the like hung on the walls. Two microphones were in the middle of the room, but other than that it was cavernous with miles of quiet space. Isabel smiled and held her breath without knowing as she opened the door to let herself in. The room smelled new and fresh, and was cool.

Isabel turned around, studying every facet of the room. A small window overlooked another building but other than that, it was all hers. "Could I work in here?" she asked. She'd never been inside a real studio before. She thought she'd be nervous, feel out of place, but she found she'd never felt more at home.

"Be my guest," May said, smiling. "I'm just going to do some work in the control room over here."

"Thanks," Isabel said, returning her smile.

She set her bag on the floor and took out her note-book, and the page from the song Spencer had begun. She'd done some work on it last night, just as she'd promised, and now she looked at her writing next to his, studied how differently they wrote, but how it all blended nonetheless. She still liked how it all came together and the thought of actually singing that with him, seeing him later, sent butterflies charging through her stomach and chest.

She just wasn't sure about the end. She was never good at endings. Maybe Spencer could help her with that one. She took out another song, one she'd also started the night before and took a look at it. She sighed, stretching out on the soft carpet.

It was a song about promises broken before they were made and alluded to storm clouds that never brought forth rain.

She read over it several times and still couldn't quite make a decision on it. That's when she cursed under her breath and heard Spencer say, behind her, "Problem?"

She jumped into a sitting position, whipped around. "Oh, hi," she said. "Sorry. I was just looking over a little something I wrote last night. I didn't know anyone else was here."

She made a move to rise, but he waved her back down.

"I'll leave you to it if you want," he said, turning to leave.

"Oh, no," she said a little too loudly, almost jumping up again.

"You sure?" he asked, half-smiling.

"Yeah," she said. She tucked her hair behind her ear. "Yeah."

"I come here sometimes to work," he said as he sat on the floor Indian style, and began tinkering with his guitar. "Quiet, nice. Good for when I'm not so…inspired."

He rolled his eyes as he said the last part and Isabel smiled. She watched him a minute. She'd found the video of him and the rest of the band on YouTube last night, had watched him over and over again, with his hair long and unruly as it was now, in jeans and a dark shirt, an un-buttoned one over that. Thomas had been right. It was like he was a different person, but still the same in a way. He'd jogged languidly from one end of the stage to the next, waving to the cheering crowd. There were so many people.

He'd clapped over his head a few times and stomped out the rhythm Greg was drumming behind him before turning into the microphone, strumming his guitar and beginning the song all in one movement. He moved about, into and around the microphone, still stomping and kicking the rhythm Greg drummed out, throwing his hair out of his face and smiling over at someone playing backup guitar.

The crowd loved it. He stepped back, played the guitar just like he owned it when he wasn't singing, and when the song slowed, he moved down over his guitar as he finished his strings and then threw it over his back and took the microphone with one hand and there was the velvet husk of night again in his voice. No wonder they loved him, Isabel thought.

He didn't just sing the song. He felt it, lived it. Singing these songs in front of these people—it was what he was meant to do. How fortunate to have found it so young. When it was over, he pushed his hair out of his eyes and smiled and waved once to the crowd, sweat gleaming over his forehead. The video ended abruptly right after that.

Isabel was still watching, still thinking of him in front of those people as he now finished tuning his guitar before her, set it aside and stretched back, putting his hands behind him on the floor. He really was striking, she thought. And it a way that had nothing to do with his good looks. She kept looking at him, he at her, a second too long. He nodded at her notebook.

"What is it? That you're working on, I mean."

"Oh." She turned, looked at her notebook a beat before turning back, her turn to roll her eyes. "It's a new song, or was. I don't know. Think I'm going to scrap it. Hey, I did work on that one you gave me yesterday."

He nodded once, held out his hand. "Let's see."

She picked up the paper, looked it over again. She'd heard all of the songs he'd written for the band on their last album, and all of them had been great. Of course, she didn't like her own words, even when she was done with them, and hated the sound of them out loud. How could she let someone else, someone whose work she admired, read them before she even got to the point where she was satisfied with them?

But there was something in those dark blue eyes, the way he automatically asked for her words, reached for her paper to hand to him. This was a job to him, something he worked at and on, like other people do with their own jobs. He wasn't any more embarrassed than a welder or a librarian or a line worker at a plastics factory. He would probably be straightforward like any experienced trainer would be about their trainee's work, but not cruel. Isabel placed the paper in his outstretched hand. What the hell?

Despite that thought, her heart started pumping as she saw his eyes moving over her words. He didn't give her any indication of whether he liked it or not. She brought a hand to her mouth, began gnawing on a nail as she watched him. Hundreds of years passed before he finally spoke without looking up.

"I like this first part, especially," he said, pointing.

She looked over at the paper. He moved a little closer, brought the paper before her eyes so she could see. She recognized what he was talking about, but was more distracted by the fresh smells of earth and cedar on him. She had to close her eyes just a second, turn her head to keep from drifting even closer to him. When she turned her head back, her cheek just brushed the edge of his hair. And yup, it was just as soft as she'd remembered from a couple of nights ago.

Isabel shook her head, was two steps away from slapping herself across the face. *Get ahold of yourself!* She cleared her throat, sat up straight, and moved away just a tad so she could concentrate.

"Yeah," she agreed, nodding. "But I think my lyrics kind of go to crap after that."

He held up a finger, shaking it slightly in disagreement as he still looked at her words. "It does get a little less...but not crappy. Not at all." He pointed to a lower part on the page. "Here, you recapture the emotion."

"Oh, but—" she started.

The thoughts at the bottom were just random, not even meant to be part of the song. But, he set her paper down and picked up his guitar. She didn't move.

He began strumming a few chords, a slow, easy melody meant, she suddenly realized, for their words. She moved to sit across. Only then did he look at her, half-smile.

He nodded once. "Go ahead and sing."

"What, now?" she asked, scrambling, turning the page of the paper.

"Uh-uh-uh," he said, stopping a moment to take the paper, toss it behind him. "You know your words. I know mine. Sing when the moment hits you."

He started to play again and she swallowed, shaking her head and looking all around. This wasn't how she usually worked. She usually wrote out her music, heard it a thousand times in her head before she heard it out loud.

"Relax," he said, smiling at her again. "Breathe."

She giggled to herself, trying to obey, but it was hard with that damn beautiful smile of his. He began to sing his own words as he strummed, and she closed her eyes, shut everything else out, his voice notwithstanding, just let the music in until she could feel her words come forth, then could hear herself sing them.

Somehow she just knew when to sing with him, when to let him sing on his own, just like he did for her. She let his guitar, his voice guide her, could feel her head nodding easily with the rhythm, felt the words coming slowly, but steadily, and he brought her and the song back home, down to earth.

When she opened her eyes to look at him, everything was different. The sun was brighter, streaming in from the window, the brush strokes of paint on the walls more defined. He nodded, continuing to half-smile in approval.

"Wow," she said. "I haven't had that much fun working on a song—" *Ever.*

"That was good," he said, still nodding to her.

She smiled, though her gratitude had nothing to do with his words of praise.

"That *was* good," she agreed. "We should get that down."

He turned once to look at May standing with her arms crossed, staring at them from behind that window. He nodded once to her and she nodded back before pressing a button on the panel.

"We already did," he said. "Hope you don't mind."

Isabel could feel a different type of shock move through her this time. "What?" she asked, standing. "We just recorded a *song*?"

"Hope you don't mind." Spencer cringed slightly. "I just saw you in here working and it looked like the wheels were turning pretty steadily. It's always been my experience that that's the best time to just go ahead and record."

Isabel brought her hands to her mouth.

"I'm sorry," he said. "I should have asked. I can tell May to ax it if you want."

He was about to make a motion to May when Isabel stopped him.

"No!" she exclaimed, giggling as excitement and exhilaration coursed through her. "I mean, we actually recorded a *song*! I can't believe it! Can we hear it, like, now?"

"Yeah, sure, let's go listen," he said, moving to open the door. He put a hand on the small of her back and let her go out before him. He stood behind her, leaning against the control panel as May pressed the button and the sound of Spencer's guitar and then their voices filled the room. Isabel brought her hands over her mouth again and could feel herself turn red as she smiled and giggled. May laughed at her, but Isabel had to admit, they did sound good together. She turned, still red and laughing, to Spencer when it ended and he touched her shoulder playfully with his own.

"You're going to have to get used to hearing the sound of your own voice."

Isabel shook her head. "I don't think I can."

She turned back to him and they laughed together a second longer until their laughs faded to smiles. Yes, Isabel thought. She was home, all right. For the first time, she was right where she was supposed to be in life.

They were still looking at one another when the door opened slowly, almost timidly. They all turned at once to see a small, twenty-ish girl with long, curly blonde hair peek in. She saw May first. Isabel could feel Spencer falter behind her.

"Hi," the girl said to May. "My name's Anna. John, your husband, I think, let me in. I'm looking for—" The girl's eyes turned, then, and landed on Spencer.

"Spence!" She laughed, threw the door open the rest of the way and came running over to him. She threw her arms around him, almost knocking Isabel out of the way. Isabel could only watch as the girl giggled again and kissed Spencer like they'd been kissing all their lives.

"Where've you been?" she squealed. "I've been calling you."

Isabel didn't even exist as Spencer nodded, smiling

to the girl. She kept knocking against Isabel as she jumped around like an excited puppy, so Isabel slipped out of the way and told May she was heading to that roof. She all of a sudden needed some air. Or a place to scream.

If she'd stayed in the room a second later, she would've seen Spencer trying, gently, to pull away from Anna, and take her arms off of his neck. But when he looked up again, Isabel was already down the hall, walking up the stone steps to the roof.

The top of the building was flat, a bit gravelly, Isabel noticed. It was breezy, and her hair automatically blew behind her. The brick surrounding the edge of the building stretched up to her chest. She went to the far edge, away from the door, and stood with her palms flat on the brick before her. She could hear distant sounds of traffic and people below, but other than that it was pretty quiet. The sun shone, warming her, though it was still cool enough that she was glad she'd chosen her white ribbed turtleneck over jeans.

Isabel sighed, closed her eyes as she turned her face up to the sun, letting it blind her momentarily. But it couldn't send away the image of that girl throwing her arms around Spencer and kissing him like it was the most natural thing in the world for her to do. Spencer hadn't put up much of a fight, either. Or had he? Isabel had been so taken aback by the whole scene that she'd just fled.

So was that it? Was Thomas actually right? Isabel

wondered as she heard a car horn below. That girl, who-ever she was, really seemed to think she and Spencer were a couple. She liked him a lot, Isabel could tell. So, why had he talked to Isabel the way he had, brought her to him and danced with her, written a song about her and sung it with her? Was that how he worked through his conquests?

Isabel wasn't entirely dumb. She read about and heard about men—singers—who had one fling after an-other, especially on the road. And once they were done, they moved on, sometimes before ending the previous relationship. And it was clear that whatever relationship he had with the giggling blonde downstairs wasn't over to her. So, why had he put the moves on Isabel?

She slapped the brick before her as she brought her face back down to look at the horizon of the town square across from her. She'd never realized how tall the crepe myrtles were. She could see the tips of them just below. If she reached far enough, she could just touch them. Isa-bel shook her head.

It was funny what one didn't see, what was there all the time. She thought about what Thomas had said about Spencer. How women loved him and how he loved them right back. Then she saw how Spencer looked at her, smiled at her, laughed with her.

She thought about how she felt when she was around him, nervous and happy as a schoolgirl, but natural and at home at the same time. He could see how she felt and he liked it. And Isabel could hardly blame that girl if Spencer had made her feel the way Isabel had felt only a few moments before.

Isabel sighed and put her chin on her palm as another breeze picked up. How could he do that? She brought her hands down, laced her fingers together. Was Thomas right? He did know the man much better than Isabel did, she conceded.

"But it didn't *seem* that way," she muttered out loud as she thought about their time together.

She sighed again. Maybe it was better that it happened now. If she had really gone and fallen full force for Spencer, like she still felt on the edge of doing, even now, it would've been that much harder for her to go in and work with him every day. She didn't know if she could do that.

The scratch she felt, seeing him with that girl, was just that—a scratch. It wasn't a deep scar like it would've been had she really been in love.

And a scratch healed much quicker than a scar, she admitted.

"Just go to work and guard your heart," she repeated one of Kat's old philosophies.

"What was that?" a familiar voice called from behind.

Isabel whipped around, saw Thomas approaching, hands in the pockets of his khakis.

"Oh, hi," she said. "Nothing. Just—weird habit of talking to myself."

"Hmm," he said, coming up beside her and placing an elbow on the brick. He looked out over the buildings for a long moment. Isabel wasn't sure how she felt about him being there when she needed this time to think and wonder. He didn't move for a while, even when he said, "May let me hear that song you and Spencer did."

He didn't look at her when he said it. His voice was little more than monotone.

"Oh?" she asked. He didn't seem entirely happy so she felt the need to clean something up. "I didn't know she was recording it until after."

"No, it was good," he cut her off. "We might end up using it, just as it is."

Isabel nodded. He still didn't seem all that happy, still focused on the buildings in the distance rather than her, but she nonetheless said, "Thanks."

"Yeah," he said.

"Hope no boundaries were overstepped," she said, feeling herself turn red again.

Thomas looked at her then, half-smiled, shook his head. He looked thoughtful, and she saw that same young man she'd asked to dance the night before.

"You think he'd take his girlfriend somewhere else," he said, and then she knew why he was acting the way he was. It had nothing to do with her or the song.

"Spencer?" she asked. Thomas nodded.

"He's still down there?" she asked.

Thomas rolled his eyes and put his palms on the brick before him.

"Practically making out with her in the lounge. Wish he'd do that shit somewhere else."

Isabel looked away from Thomas, blinked several times. "Making out?" she repeated. Thank God she'd come to the roof when she had. Not a sight she would've wanted to see.

"Mmm," he said, confirming. "He's not exactly the most professional of people."

She swallowed hard, barely hearing Thomas's words. Why had Spencer been so…flirtatious, nice, whatever, when he had a girlfriend?

"You all right?" Thomas suddenly asked.

She looked back at him, forcing herself back into reality, and nodded. "Thanks," she said, though in her mind she was thanking him for far more than him asking if she was okay. She was thanking him for warning her before she went and made a big mistake.

She supposed in a way she was thanking Spencer, too, because now she suddenly knew what she was going to write about next.

Chapter 8

December 11, 2016:

At eight that morning, Isabel finally drove the couple of miles to Kat's house. Like the town square, Isabel noticed, all of the houses lining the little hill on which Kat lived all looked the same.

When she pulled into the driveway that circled around the back of the house, she found herself a little nervous. *Calm down*, she scolded herself as she grabbed her duffle bag. *It's just Kat who loves you and practically raised you your whole life.*

She made her way up the back steps and unlocked the door. The back porch still held the washer and dryer and opened into the kitchen. The smell of coffee immediately greeted Isabel and she was glad for it. She'd never been so in need of a cup in her life. Other than that, the house was quiet.

Isabel took in the wooden cabinets and wood paneling on the wall, the ancient beige refrigerator and noticed that Kat still kept a cup on top of it so she could fix her water throughout the day. Isabel smiled as she dropped her bag on the brown and yellow linoleum floor in the kitchen and fixed a cup of coffee before shedding her coat and draping it over one of the chairs in the dining room that was adjacent to the kitchen.

She looked in the closed-in side porch that had been Isabel's room there. Windows still lined the expanse of the room and it was still as bright and white as it had ever been. Her little double bed with the purple butterfly quilt still sat off to one side, as did the oak dresser and ancient television that had been her grandmother's.

Isabel smiled, her nervousness subsiding at the sight of her old room. She got her coat and bag and dropped them on her bed.

The wood floor creaked underneath her feet as she made her way around the living room at the front of the house, looking at the pictures of all of their various family members in old frames on the walls and tables amongst Tiffany lamps and knickknacks so old they were considered antiques.

She passed the black and white tiled bathroom with

its etched glass shower door, the back bedroom with its Earth tones that had been Kat's son's and Kat's darkened bedroom beside it before coming to the one that had been Kat's daughter's—done completely in yellow shag carpeting and paint.

To this day, they didn't call it Serena's room. They called it the yellow bedroom. Isabel laughed out loud in the silence of the home as she remembered one of the first stories Kat had ever told Isabel about the house when she'd moved in...

It was night and Serena was just a baby, sleeping in her crib. Kat had been going to check on her when she saw someone at the window of Serena's room, trying to pry open the screen. She'd immediately dropped to the floor, crawled across floor to the kitchen, and took the phone to call the police. She had to count the numbers on the rotary in the darkness, but she got the police, told them what was happening, and they said they would send someone right away. As she began crawling back, she heard someone say, "Don't move, or I'll shoot!"

She looked up in time to see her husband, Duncan, standing in the doorway of Serena's room, pointing his finger in the assailant's direction, obviously hoping his hand looked like a gun and that the person would freeze, but it didn't work. The person ran away and, when Kat told the police the whole story later, all the while trying to calm Serena, who was still screaming from Duncan having startled her awake, they didn't believe her. After a near arrest for faking an emergency, Kat managed to convince them of her story.

"What's so funny?" a voice behind Isabel startled her and she nearly dropped her coffee. She turned to see Kat, smiling and holding a bag from the local bakery, all done up in her bright red lipstick and gold earrings. Never leave the house without your lipstick or your earrings, she always said.

Isabel forgot everything and hugged her cousin. She found herself holding onto Kat for longer than usual, realizing how long it had been since they'd seen one another—almost a year this time.

"I was hoping to be back before you got here," Kat said, turning, her arm still around Isabel's shoulders. "Come on, I got us some goodies to have while you tell me everything that's been going on."

That sat together in Kat's open dining room, drinking coffee and eating butter rum muffins in front of the picture window that overlooked the back garden and let in the delicate morning sun. Isabel just immediately went into seeing Spencer that very morning.

"You're sure it was him?" Kat asked, taking another sip from her mug.

"I'm sure," Isabel said. *I could feel him there before I even saw him.*

"Well, why in the world didn't you call out to him?" Kat leaned forward, her head down and eyes upturned, but she laughed when Isabel did.

I'm not sure I want to see him, any of them, Isabel thought, remembering her heart pounding when she saw him, the tears she hadn't even known had welled up in her eyes.

But Kat's reaction was only natural. She didn't know how it all ended between Spencer and Isabel and hadn't asked. She only knew that it had.

It was almost eleven when they moved to the living room. Isabel unpacked a few things and sat with Kat, watching television while Kat read the latest Debbie Macomber. Isabel didn't remember much after that, only waking to find the sun a little dimmer, the day a little darker.

"Well, I was wondering if you were going to sleep through the night," Kat said, playfully slapping Isabel's leg. Isabel uncurled herself, stiff from the tight position she'd kept, and stretched. She asked what time it was.

"A little after five," Kat said, and Isabel jumped and looked at the red digital numbers on the clock that sat above the television.

"Wow," Isabel said and rubbed her eyes.

She looked down and put her head in her hands, rubbing her eyes again to wake up. She'd dreamed about Spencer, just like she knew she would. They'd been at the beach, walking together, saying very little until he just wasn't there anymore.

Then the day had turned gray and dark. Isabel had tried to run, but she always seemed to move so slowly in her dreams. She couldn't outrun the storm in her dream, and never could find Spencer, either.

As Kat went to the bathroom, Isabel walked out to her room, found her notebook in her duffel bag and started scribbling about storms and the beach and disappearances. Loss. She'd just finished and closed the book in one hand when Kat came up behind, asked if she wanted to try out the new Japanese restaurant on the square. Isabel felt a rumbling in her stomach and realized just how hungry she was.

"I'd *love* to," she said.

They ate Hibachi shrimp and chicken with broccoli and fried rice until they were beyond full, and so later, they took a walk in the crisp December evening. Isabel was quiet during the walk and the ride home, and Kat didn't question it. She knew, as quiet as Isabel already was, she became quieter when she got nervous, and needed that time with her own thoughts to work through it.

Isabel hugged her cousin before closing the door to the side porch and shutting the blinds. She turned the television on but muted it, just let the gentle glow be a constant while she dressed for bed and the climbed in under the quilt and turned on her side toward the wall.

Tomorrow was it. Spencer, Thomas, the rest of them—she was going to see them and there was no hiding this time. Unless, of course, she just backed out and stayed home.

She turned over in bed, watching a car's headlights

shine out across her ceiling as it passed by on the road, considering. It was tempting to stay away, anonymous and afar, to disappear. She was good at that. Maybe she would.

Chapter 9

November 2009:

I think you two should do this one together, just the two of you," Thomas said over a month later to Isabel and Spencer. Isabel was sitting on the stool in front of the mic and Spencer was lying on the floor, one arm thrown over his eyes. It was close to eleven at night and they'd all been at the studio since nine that morning.

That was how it had been almost each day. Thomas had everyone come in at ten by the latest. He used the song Spencer and Isabel did as it was, and Isabel was grateful. She was too embarrassed, hurt, whatever, to look at Spencer, much less sing with him again, though there were times she and Thomas or she and Renee were doing backup on a song of his or he was doing backup on a song of hers and she could feel him looking at her.

But on everything else, Thomas was a hard ass. He thought nothing of stopping in the middle of a song five or six times and demanding everyone start over or scraping what they spent the better part of a day on. Not that it didn't pay off. She had to admit, the two songs Thomas let her contribute to the album sounded better than she thought could by the time he and Spencer and May were done with them in the control room. She rehearsed and recorded and then re-recorded lyrics in the little isolation booth all by herself, just like Thomas made everyone do, even himself.

At first she had to close her eyes while singing, but it got better after a few days. That second day she did the re-recordings, she opened her eyes to find Thomas standing with his arms folded, grimacing at the controls May was sitting over as they scrutinized her voice. Spencer was seated, the side of his face resting on his fist as he looked at her. When their eyes met, he gave her that half smile and she looked away. She felt the strain in her voice and knew they'd scrap that take also, but Thomas told her after that it was the best recording yet and that was the one they were going to use.

When she wasn't needed, she would drop down in one of the chairs in the lounge to read one of the books she'd brought or work on the scarf she'd started knitting, but she would find her throat tight and tired, her fingers nearly raw from playing the guitar in all the takes and her eyes too heavy to do anything but close.

Between the constant rehearsals and practicing the band's songs from the first album to get them down before they went on tour in a couple of months, she was past exhausted.

Thomas told her she would be playing bass and doing a lot of backup singing on the songs from that album, but he wanted her more at the forefront when they did songs for this next one and would bring in one of their substitute bassists for the songs on that one.

"Your voice is good," he said to her one afternoon. "I'd like to showcase it."

Despite her exhaustion, she was thrilled, and she had to admit on the phone one evening to Kat. She didn't want to do anything else with her time.

"Well, I'm proud of you, darlin,'" Kat had said sleepily into the phone that night. "But you know, I have to say, you don't seem all that happy. Is everything all right?"

Isabel closed her eyes. She knew she'd have to tell Kat everything eventually and so she just spilled it then and there, everything about recording the song with Spencer and how everything seemed to be going so great until the moment the blonde girl showed up and staked her claim on him, and then Thomas's explanation and her ultimate avoidance of Spencer.

"You haven't asked him who that girl is?" Kat's voice was alert now.

"I don't know, I just—"

"Clammed up and withdrew?" Kat's voice wasn't unkind, but it was knowing. That was Isabel's defense when she felt hurt.

"He's tried to get my attention," Isabel admitted.

"Well, you're going to be spending a lot more time with him. You can't be silent with him forever. And I'll tell you something else, too."

"What?"

"Your voice changed when you mentioned his name."

"Okay, I admit, I still have feelings for him," Isabel said, dropping back onto her bed. "But how can I when Thomas so obviously does for me? And after everything he said about Spencer—what am I supposed to do?"

"Well, honey, if it bothers you, talk to Spencer."

"I already wrote a song about it."

Kat laughed. "Of course you did. But seriously, talk to him if you're bothered."

Isabel examined her nails in the dark.

"Do you like Thomas?"

"Mmm, yeah, sure. He's nice. No fireworks yet, but I don't see him ever hurting me."

"Nice," Kat repeated.

Isabel had to laugh. But she made a decision at that moment, though, almost instantaneously. She was going to like Thomas, was going to spend more time with him. Spencer had his other girl. He had many, according to Thomas.

And she'd done good with all but avoiding him for the past several weeks. Until now. Until Thomas stood there, studying the lyrics to a song and telling Isabel and Spencer do it together.

"I don't know," Isabel began.

Thomas silenced her when his head shot up and he looked right at her, challenging her to continue. Spencer languidly rubbed his eyes and sat up.

"You sure it'll work as a duet?" was all the protest he gave Thomas.

He yawned. Isabel looked down. She knew by now that that was the way he did things, so unlike the strict way Thomas did. He made his concerns heard, usually through a question like that. If a mix or a chorus or a harmony didn't work, that's usually all he had to do—ask a question about how it would and then it would be fixed. He'd done that on one of her songs when she couldn't get the melody right.

He hadn't said much at all, just walked over to the other side of the room, took a mandolin from the shelf— was there anything he couldn't play?—to play during the song, had Greg switch to brush sticks, and, when they were finished, said, "Think that would work?"

They finished recording the song within a half hour after having spent five days trying to figure it out. Isabel suddenly wondered how quickly they could finish an album if Spencer were in charge.

"Up to you to make it happen," Thomas said, handing his lyrics to his friend. Spencer took them without a word and looked at them. Even he knew when to throw it in and hand it to Spencer. "Work on it, we'll pick up tomorrow," Thomas continued. "Everybody go on home, get some rest, it's late. We'll start fresh at noon tomorrow."

Isabel sat on the stool, still stunned into silence as she thought about Thomas's demand that she sing, yet again, with Spencer. She still sat there long after everyone gathered up their things and started clearing out. Spencer tossed her a look as he left but she didn't look back at him and he didn't press her.

Every time she saw him coming down the hall or in the lounge or wherever, she always doubled back, finding another place to occupy. As a result, they'd barely said two words to each other in the past weeks. And now, she certainly didn't want to sing with him. Because if she did, if she gave in—

"You all right?" Thomas's voice brought her back.

She got up, started putting her papers and her knitting in her bag, her guitar in its case. "Sorry," she said, still packing up. Thomas made a move to leave. "Um," she said.

He stopped, looked right at her.

"About singing again with Spencer—"

Thomas cut her off. "You guys sound great together. That duet you guys did? That's already a hit, I can tell. Everyone can. Even Greg said it was awesome."

Isabel felt herself smile. Greg said little to nothing, though he didn't have to. The boy could play the drums like no one's business.

"And when he did backup on your song and you on his, well, that's all they needed to make them awesome."

She laughed, stretching and running her hands through her hair. "So why'd you have us re-record them sixteen times?"

"Because I know what I'm doing and I know one take is never enough."

He crossed the room until he was right in front of her, didn't miss a beat as he took her face in his hands and kissed her. Isabel had to stop herself from jumping backward. It was the first time he'd ever done that.

"Look, I know it was a little weird with him when that girl came running in and almost ruined that first session, but hey, she's gone now," he said when he released her. "They broke up. And your voice is meant to sing with his. Your voice may be his but you—you're meant to be with me. You're mine."

Isabel didn't speak. She didn't breathe. She let him kiss her again, though she didn't return it, not naturally, anyway. She didn't even close her eyes. And when he opened his to look at her again, he reached up and ran the back of his hand over her hair, down her face and to her neck, almost as if she were a rare creature that fascinated him. She could feel a tightening twist in her bottom of her throat. What was happening here?

She turned away. She didn't like the idea of possessiveness. What she liked was talking to him about music, seeing the way his expertise made certain songs better. And he did know what he was talking about. She knew she and Spencer sounded good together, like it was almost like their voices were made to sing together. But every time she did, every time she heard their voices in the speakers, hell, every time he looked at her, she felt the edge of that cliff again.

And she couldn't help it, either. She would find herself watching him as he re-recorded his own lyrics, one hand over his headphones. His voice carried a slight Southern accent. She hadn't noticed that before. It gave his songs a casual, laid back feel.

It was the kind of music people could listen to while taking a long drive in a convertible or dance to in a small town country bar.

Isabel pulled a paper from her bag and turned back to Thomas right now. She didn't say a word as she took it over to the piano and seated herself in front of it.

"This is something I wrote a long time ago," she said.

Some people think five weeks is a long time, she thought, so she didn't consider it a complete lie. But, she didn't want him to get an idea in his head.

She played slow, long notes, letting each carry before moving on to the next, sang her words to Spencer, though Thomas couldn't know.

She described fire and dark blue flickers of light, what Spencer could be to her in that moment, dreams in a lovely winter. She sang of the singe of seeing someone else, someone young and lovely, enter the picture.

She asked the questions she wanted to ask, gave descriptions of her running away before an answer could be heard.

She brought in the deeper notes as she told him, her listener, what he could be to her, how much she could love him if he would have let her, and, ultimately, what had to be in the now and even the future, but how she knew he wasn't going to forget her.

Isabel finished the song, happy, even if Thomas didn't use it. She had originally worded the last lyrics as being she would never forget him, but changed them on a dime when singing in front of Thomas and was glad she had. This gave her a bit of a victory at the end.

Isabel looked at Thomas after a minute. He didn't show much emotion, the way Spencer did when he nodded his head to songs and really got into them in the control room and isolation booth. Thomas just grimaced.

"I love it," he said. "We'll use it on this album. Let's do it now."

Isabel sat up straighter, raised her eyebrows.

He put together a little demo of the song for her to

sing to, and though she recorded her lyrics in about thirty minutes, it was nearly one in the morning when Thomas closed the door behind them and locked it.

"Yeah, Spence could do a hell of guitar solo near the middle and I'm also going to put both him and Renee on backup vocals on this one," he said, putting his hands in his pockets as he walked alongside her. He'd been walking her home nearly every night. "Keep the piano, too. I'll have Greg use brush sticks again. I'll let them hear it in the morning and we should actually have it finished up by the end of the day. Looks like we should have the whole album done soon."

"You think it's going okay?" she asked, her breath coming out as smoke when she spoke. She shivered.

"I think it is going to blow the first one out of the water," he said. He spoke slowly, emphasizing each word.

Wow, Isabel thought inwardly. What if he was right? She tried not to let too many possibilities enter her mind as she thought about it.

"I love your imagery," he said, bringing her back to him. "Especially revisiting the fire element."

It was Isabel's turn to grimace.

"First line," he said, singing it to her as a reminder, and then pointed out how she used the burn she felt when she'd been hurt.

"Oh, I didn't realize that," she said, seeing her words with new eyes.

"I don't want to pry, but I think you really loved that man you wrote this about."

Isabel blinked.

"And so, I'm glad it was from a long time ago."

They got to her door and he kissed her again, the side of her face this time. Isabel closed her eyes, but at least she didn't jerk her head away. What was happening? She didn't know and couldn't figure it out as she walked up the stairs to her apartment. But she could sure feel him watching her as she walked away from him.

Chapter 10

December 12, 2016:

At five the next evening, Spencer took the steps down from the loft and fixed the tallest black coffee they sold. He told Scott, his manager, he wouldn't be there tonight and left it up to him to close the place, tossing him the spare keys as he left. Scott took them with only a little surprise, told him he'd see him later in the week.

They didn't have to be at the studio until five-thirty, but he'd been up since just after dawn. He still only clocked in about four or five hours of sleep every night. He hadn't always been that way. He could sleep until noon sometimes when he was a kid. It was moving to his uncle's ranch that changed that habit really quick. He remembered his uncle coming in and banging on his door at five in the morning, throwing on the lights, even opening the window if it was cold outside to get his seemingly unwakeable nephew to rise and help him bring the horses in from the pasture, feed and water them, get started on any one of the million projects that needed doing that day.

Spencer paused a split second after opening the heavy glass door and leaving the warm aroma of coffee. He looked at the little door beside the shop that still held strong between the coffee shop and a gift shop. He didn't live in the apartment that Isabel had lived in all those years ago. It didn't seem right. It had been a long time— six years—since he'd walked through that door to the cozy loft area that Isabel, his Isabel, had called home. Yet, every time he passed by the place, he stopped, almost without knowing or thinking, and remembered the time they'd shared there.

He sighed, walking into the frigid air. He was surprised to find himself nervous, as it wasn't his custom to be so. He took a long sip of his coffee. Coffee always had a different type of effect on him. It could wake him but could also steady his nerves. And that was just what he needed right now—steady alertness.

The studio was just down the street, so he took his time walking. It was quiet, even at that hour, when a lot of people were getting off work. The day was clear, the sun cold as it shone down through the trees that lined even the town streets. Spencer supposed that was one reason he came back to Laurel Springs. He could breathe here, focus here, unlike in the big cities where the exhaust and car horns and shouts and jostling from people all around made it hard to even see, much less think.

Plus, Laurel Springs was where he'd met her, Isabel. It was her hometown, a place she might return. He'd never sought her out, despite moving back, had decided long ago that if they were indeed meant to be together, they would meet again by happenstance.

Spencer stopped in front of the small, two-story brick building that housed the studio. He looked at his watch, saw that he was still fifteen minutes early. He took another sip of his coffee, thought about waiting, so he could see her come from afar, if she even decided to come. He looked around, no one around. Meeting again like this wasn't exactly what he'd had in mind when he'd thought happenstance. But, at the same time, he wasn't all that surprised that Thomas had reached out now, on the band's anniversary.

He'd always said that out of all the places they'd recorded, this place had the best acoustics out of any of them. The album they'd made after Spencer and Isabel had left had barely charted into the 80s and the one Thomas had done solo hadn't charted at all. Music was Thomas's life, everything he'd worked for. He didn't know how to do anything else, and he'd die before he stopped making music. That was why Spencer and Isabel were back.

Shiloh Ridge had seen its greatest success when Isabel had joined, given over her lovely words and voice that sang largely with Spencer's. It hadn't surprised anyone how well they harmonized. Except Thomas.

Spencer pushed back the thick hair that had fallen over his forehead, took one last look around, and pushed his way inside a second before Isabel rounded the corner, walking quickly, her head down, one hand on her messenger bag, the other holding a largely untouched cup of coffee.

Kat had told her to relax, that she had this, that she was as talented as she had ever been. Isn't that why they were calling her back? Hadn't that band had their biggest success while she'd been a part of it? Though Isabel had answered yes to all of the questions, and had relaxed in the few seconds that followed their conversation, she still had to walk the mile to the studio in town and even after that, was still a tight ball of nothing but nerves.

She walked right past the door of the studio at first, had to turn around to place her hand on the metal knob. But for some reason, that's when she stopped, when the nerves that had been so wound up decided to open. She felt a small shake in her chest and let go of the knob. No one was around, so she could have her freak-out moment all to herself, thank goodness.

She breathed in, placed a hand on her stomach, but still felt something rising in her chest and had to close her eyes and turn around once more and face the street.

Something strange happened in that moment, though, as she opened her eyes. The nerves closed up but unraveled, her shoulders dropped with ease. She remembered things, songs she'd sung and the thunderous applause after, songs she'd written long after she'd left—in short, things she still had, that had never been lost. Shiloh Ridge—Thomas—may still own the rights to them, but they were hers. They always would be. They were the things she'd completed and contributed to the world, things that she loved.

This going in and facing everyone, it was going to happen. Not only for her, but for Spencer and Thomas, too. There was nothing—no amount of nervousness of fear—that could stop it. Nothing could prolong the wait.

Isabel brought her coffee to her lips and drank, felt the warmth and the caffeine and the milk make their way into her body. She didn't hesitate a second time when she grasped the doorknob before her and pushed it forward.

Chapter 11

November 10, 2009:

The next day Isabel turned twenty-five. Kat wanted to take her to dinner, but Isabel didn't know how long Thomas would keep them that day, so she said she didn't know, but that she would definitely call to set up a time later if she had to stay at the studio.

At the studio. Isabel smiled inwardly to herself as she repeated the phrase in her mind, walking to that very place that crisp November morning. It was still colder than it had been, the promise of a bitter winter on the way. But it was refreshing instead of biting and skin-splitting, she thought. Frost glistened on every surface and the sun shone from a cerulean blue sky. Isabel didn't know if it was the catharsis of her song last night, her exhaustion, or doing something she loved day in and day out, but everything felt beautiful, she thought.

"Isabel!"

Isabel was still smiling to herself when she turned to see Renee waving to her from down the street. Isabel smiled and waved back.

"Hey, Renee," she said when she got up to the studio door.

"Hey," Renee returned. "Man, it is *freezing* again, isn't it?"

"Yeah, it is," Isabel said. "You want to go on in with me?"

"I'll be in in a minute, I have to pick something up. I just saw you from across the street and wanted to say hi." Renee giggled as she spoke, the way she did a lot of times. It was probably her already good mood, but Isabel couldn't help but laugh with her.

"I'm glad you did," Isabel said. And she was. She liked Renee. She was a vibrant presence among the quiet seriousness of everyone else.

"So how're you liking everything so far?" Renee asked, pushing her bangs off her forehead. "I know Thomas can be a bit tough."

"Oh, but he's great at what he does," Isabel said. "Everyone is. I was just thinking how I love every minute of it even though we work such long hours."

"I'm glad," Renee said, her pretty brown eyes widening and dancing. "Not just because it's been so hard to find someone since Jess left but also because your songs are great. Your voice is lovely, too. Soft but powerful and your songs—you write about things that a lot of people, especially women, can relate to."

Isabel felt her face blush and she looked at the ground. "Thank you. I really feel like I'm where I belong."

"It seems like Spencer has finally met his match, too."

Isabel jerked her head back in Renee's direction. "What?"

"Your voice. It's a great match for his. None of us ever thought we'd find someone who'd be able to match the veracity of his."

"Veracity," Isabel repeated.

Renee laughed a little again and shrugged. "That's what I like to call it, anyway. There's such a realness, a truth in the way he sings. I don't know how else to describe it."

"No, I like it," Isabel assured her. "And I agree. I'm just not sure if I'm his match. I mean, I don't know if I feel comfortable singing with him on a regular basis."

Renee blinked and tilted her head, waiting for Isabel to continue.

"Well, it's just—" Isabel began, but suddenly felt like she'd said too much, gone too far. She wished she hadn't said anything at all. Now she had to go full force and admit everything. "Well, it's just something Thomas told me," she said.

"Thomas?" Renee said, grimacing.

Isabel sighed and shifted her weight. She tightened her grip on her bag. "I mean, yeah, but it's also something that happened after that first song he and I did together."

"That was a beautiful song," Renee said. "Damn near made me cry."

Yeah, me too. Isabel sighed and ran her hand through her hair. "Thanks, Renee," she said, and struggled to say exactly what she meant without divulging how she really felt about Spencer. "It's just something happened after."

"What happened?" Renee prompted.

"Well, a girl, Anna was her name, came in and sort of, I don't know, climbed all over him. I mean, she seemed sweet and everything—"

"It kind of ruined the chemistry that was needed to sing a duet," Renee said, nodding knowingly.

"More or less."

"Yeah," Renee said, still nodding. "I know. When you're recording, a duet especially, there has to be a certain chemistry. It's delicate. Little things can sometimes throw it off. I mean, Thomas steered clear, yeah, but Anna doesn't really know the dynamics."

Isabel shrugged and nodded. "I guess."

"Besides, it's not like she's his girlfriend or anything."

"Oh, I know, they broke up."

Renee looked as a car passed them by. "Oh, they were never really together, anyway."

Isabel snapped her head back to Renee's direction. "What?"

"Believe me, she wanted to be. And you've gotta give that girl credit for trying. She started flirting with him backstage at a show a few months ago."

Isabel laughed, trying to seem nonchalant. "Like a lot of girls?"

"Yeah, I guess," Renee confirmed, but shrugged. She didn't seem to be saying it happened a lot, the way Thomas had. But she wasn't elaborating, either. "Anyway, Spencer did take her out once or twice, but told us one day at the studio that they didn't really have anything in common. He tried and tried to be nice about it but she just wouldn't leave. Persistent. That girl should be an agent or something when she grows up."

"Wait," Isabel said, dropping her bag to the ground. It had suddenly become too heavy. "I thought they were making out that day she showed up at the studio."

Renee grimaced in confusion. "Making out? The day you recorded the song?"

"Yeah, that's what Thomas said. They were making out in the lounge after I went up to the roof."

Renee looked in the distance at the stone courthouse

like she was trying to make sense of something and the answer was just out there. "No, I wouldn't say that," she said. "I mean, yeah, they were in the lounge and Anna was all over him, but no, he was trying to talk to her and get her off of him. I only saw them once when I was on my way to the kitchen, but, yeah, he definitely wasn't reciprocating."

"Huh," Isabel said, turning to look at a crepe myrtle, bare except for the lights. Now it felt like she needed to search for an answer in the distance.

"But I doubt she'll be back. They talked for a long time, and then she just threw on her coat, stormed out, and told us it was nice knowing us."

"Huh," Isabel said again.

She couldn't seem to come up with anything more elaborate. Renee laughed, but Isabel wasn't able to laugh back. She was too caught in wondering why Thomas had told her Spencer and Anna were making out if that wasn't the case. Had he just misinterpreted, or been mistaken? Had Thomas and Renee just seen them at different moments?

What had happened? Had she been avoiding Spencer because of a misunderstanding? Oh, no, she'd gone and written a song about it! *Oh, shit*, she thought, remembering her lyrics in that song. He was totally going to figure everything out! And Thomas wanted him to sing, do a guitar solo, of all things! How could she have played that stupid song for Thomas?!

"Shit," she said, rubbing the back of her neck.

"What?" Renee asked. Isabel looked up. She'd almost forgotten Renee was right there.

"Oh, nothing," Isabel said, struggling to come up with something to say. "I just, um, I hope she's all right—Anna, I mean."

"Oh, I wouldn't worry about her. Greg went to Roman's to get us some take out the other night and he said she was in there with some young, long-haired hippie-looking guy."

Isabel faltered slightly. "Wow."

Renee looked at her watch. "Okay, I really do have to get to the music store now. If Greg gets here before I do, tell him I'll be right back, okay?"

"Okay," Isabel said.

Renee turned around and stopped a minute. "I liked talking with you. Let's get together, us girls, for dinner or something sometime. If Thomas lets us off the hook before ten at night, that is."

Isabel laughed and waved. "Sounds good."

She took her key and unlocked the front door. She was the first one there again, so she started the coffee in the kitchenette and drank a cup as she watched the day unfold from the window in the isolation booth and wondered what exactly she'd done last night with that song, and how she was going to un-do it. She only turned around when the door opened.

She saw Spencer emerge, messenger bag and guitar

in one hand, coffee in the other. "I used to be the first one here every day," he said in greeting.

She looked at him a second before taking a sip from her own cup. Her lyrics had been echoing in her mind since she'd spoken to Renee, but now, seeing him again, it was like they came back to her for the first time. Now they didn't seem to make sense. Isabel sighed, confused on a lot. She had just gone and believed what Thomas had told her because she was stung by seeing Anna and Spencer.

Now she just felt bewildered. And embarrassed. She could feel the blush in her skin again. She couldn't sing those words in front of Spencer, certainly not now. What on earth had she been thinking?

"You all right?" he asked after he'd set everything down, laid back on the floor and closed his eyes.

Talk to him, she could hear Kat's voice say to her again.

Finally, she came over to sit on the floor next to him. She took a breath, trying to find and gather thoughts. Her brain felt overloaded and empty at the same time. *Start simple.* "I'm good. You?"

He opened his eyes and looked over at her. He clearly hadn't expected her to come over and sit next to him, much less answer his question. He sat up. "I've been wanting to tell you I'm sorry," he said.

Aw, man! Isabel took another sip of her coffee and looked at him, hoping her thoughts didn't come through.

"For what?" she asked, and he looked at her with his head down and his eyes turned up to her, a wry look on his face that she couldn't help smiling at. "It's fine," she said.

And it was. It's not like they'd been in a relationship.

"Nonetheless," he continued. "We—Anna and I— were broken up. Hell, we were never even really together. I just, when she showed up, I was surprised, I didn't expect it, and I tried to talk with her. I just didn't want to hurt her again. Seems like I did, anyway, though." Spencer looked down at his coffee as he spoke.

"Thank you," she said, taking another sip of her own coffee. "For telling me, finally."

"Couldn't find a time. Got the feeling you were avoiding me." He pushed her shoulder playfully with his own and she smiled down at her coffee mug.

"I was a little uncomfortable," Isabel admitted. "I just, I didn't know what to do." *I'd heard one thing and now I know another.* She was suddenly angry about that. "Plus, we've been pretty busy," she said.

"We have," he agreed.

"She did seem fairly inexperienced at—love." Isabel turned her head as she took a sip of coffee. When she looked back, Spencer still had his head down but had turned his eyes up to her, along with that ironic smile again. "Like them young, do you?" she teased. She couldn't help smiling back.

Spencer laughed and took a sip of his coffee. "She's

twenty," he admitted. "Maybe she just likes hers old, ever think of that?"

Isabel slit her eyes as she studied him. "You're not old."

"You think?" Spencer set his coffee down and turned so he could face her. They stayed like that a while until they both broke into laughter.

"How old *are* you?" she asked.

He brought his coffee cup up to his mouth again and took a long sip. Instead of answering, he just shook a finger at her.

"You're seriously not going to tell me?" she asked.

"I'm thirty-four," he said, rising long enough to take off his jacket. "Oh, speaking of age," he said, remembering something all of a sudden. He drifted off as he went for his bag and began rummaging. He pulled out a slender box wrapped in brown paper and handed it to Isabel.

"What's this?" she asked, taking it. He gestured for her to open it as he took another sip of coffee and sat down, and she tore the paper away to find a sleek CD in a transparent case.

She looked at him for explanation.

"It's a recording of that first song we did a few weeks ago. My way of saying 'happy birthday.'"

Isabel's hand shot to her mouth. She didn't know what to say. "Oh, my, thank you!"

She instinctively reached to hug him and that was the moment she realized what it felt like for Spencer Logan to hold her back. He was taller, a lot stronger, but he held her gently and tucked his chin over her shoulder, just like he was protecting her from something. Isabel moved her face inward and could smell that earthy scent on him again and closed her eyes. He moved a hand up her back, took a strand of her loose hair, twisted it lightly between his fingers. Her stomach fluttered and her chest felt hot all of a sudden, her arms weak. They'd been hugging, holding onto one another a long time, she suddenly realized. She pulled away, smiled more at the floor.

"Um," she began, unable to find any thoughts except that of Spencer holding her. Nonetheless she tried. "How did you know it was my birthday?"

It was Spencer's turn to shrug. "Ben, our manager, told me."

Isabel nodded. She remembered having to give all her info to Ben so she could get paid. But still, why would Ben just give away that information? She opened her mouth to ask when he said, "Your voice is really beautiful."

Isabel looked at him, feeling a small catch in her chest. Between his niceness now and what she'd heard this morning, Isabel was having a harder and harder time staying mad at this guy.

"Thank you," she said, keeping her eyes level with his.

After a moment they smiled at one another and she told him how she felt about his.

"Thank you," he returned. They were still looking at one another, had been for a little too long, when Renee and Greg came in. They both immediately straightened and shifted around. Greg waved to all in greeting, still looking down as he shivered one last time. He didn't seem to notice anything. Renee said hi, but her eyes lingered on Isabel for a moment, trying to get her attention. Or maybe Isabel was just imagining it, she thought. She didn't know. Either way, she couldn't look at Renee.

"Hey, Spence, happy birthday," Greg said, shrugging out of his coat while Renee giddily handed him a large box.

Isabel turned to him with a dropped jaw.

"Thirty-four today." He winked at her and got up. "Thanks," he said, taking the box from Renee. "Actually, Isabel has—"

Isabel straightened and shook her head at him, pleading. He stopped, getting the message.

"…uh, has already given me her gift," he covered.

He grimaced, confused, but nonetheless nodded when she mouthed, "Thank you."

She'd explain later how she hated parties and being the center of attention. Renee sat down next to her while Spencer opened the large box and pulled out a new acoustic guitar.

"Aw, however did you know?" he asked. "Thanks."

"Wow, that's really great," Isabel said to Renee, who nodded happily.

It was obvious she'd done the choosing on Spencer's gift.

He patted Greg on the arm and reached out to hug Renee. When his eyes met Isabel's again, she mouthed, "I'm sorry. I didn't know."

He shook his head in the slightest and winked at her, freezing her for just a second.

I could really get into trouble.

"Hey, everybody, how's it going?" Thomas burst in, barely looking at anyone as he set his things down in the corner and shrugged out of his jacket. He came over and leaned down to kiss Isabel without telling her hello. She let him, though she couldn't look at Spencer when he did. She stared at Thomas.

Why did you lie to me? Did you lie to me? What happened?

"Check it out," Renee said, hopping up and gesturing toward Spencer's new guitar as if she were a model presenting a prize on *The Price Is Right*. Thomas looked over.

"Oh, hey, that's great," he said, coming over and running his hand along it. "Hey, I'm sorry I didn't get you anything. I'll get you something as soon as money's not so tight."

Spencer waved him off, still tuning his new prize. "Ah, it's fine."

"Hey, did you get a chance to work on those lyrics at all?" Thomas said, his voice loud again, as he turned back to Spencer. Spencer nodded as he began rummaging in his bag again. "And Isabel has a little something new, too, that she's going to contribute."

"Oh, I don't know," Isabel said quickly. She didn't know if she could do it anymore. She didn't feel the same as she did last night. She struggled to think of an excuse. "I'm not sure it's ready."

"It is," Thomas said. "Why're you changing your mind? You recorded the lyrics. Didn't we settle this last night? I said it was good. I said we could arrange it. Don't you remember?"

Everyone was silent as he stared at Isabel for an explanation. No one could know what she couldn't say in that moment about the song or about Spencer, not even Thomas, who knew the backstory. Part of it, anyway.

"Um—yeah—no, you're right," she stumbled, taken aback.

She turned to look through her bag for the lyrics. She blinked a few times and breathed in, trying to settle her startled nerves. She didn't know what the big deal was. They already had ten songs including the one Spencer was handing to Thomas right then.

"Come on, let's go hear it," Thomas said, motioning for everyone to come into the studio.

Isabel kept her head down as she heard herself sing the song she'd felt so good about just twelve hours ago. Now it just seemed out of place, like a bug scuttling across the surface of a freshly-baked cake. Isabel turned her eyes up to Spencer, trying to see him without looking at him, without being noticed. He didn't seem to have much reaction. He only nodded his head to the rhythm. Maybe he didn't notice how the lyrics were about him.

"And then you two would come in here, and again on the later chorus," Thomas said, pointing at the controls, telling Spencer and Renee exactly where they would sing backup on her song. Spencer kept nodding along with the rhythm.

"That emotion is awesome," he said. "I could do a guitar solo about here."

"That's what I thought, exactly!" Thomas said, slapping Spencer's arm and then putting his arm around Isabel and dragging her into a half hug.

She still hadn't said a word to him, she realized.

"Maybe you could over-sing this last part, Isabel," Spencer said when it was over, pointing at her handwritten lyrics on the paper. He looked at her. He gave no indication of knowing whether or not the song was about him.

Well, maybe I got away with it after all, she thought, coming forth to look where he was pointing.

"The emotion's raw here, intense. I think if you over-sang, it would really bring it home."

"Yeah," she said, nodding, realizing what he meant. "I think so, too. Thanks."

It took them all day to work out the rest of the song. They still had some arranging, rehearsing to do before they recorded, but overall they finished by six that night. Renee and Spencer came in at different parts on the chorus and he was right—when she over-sang and repeated phrases at the end while he and Renee kept up with the chorus, the result was the fiery sentiment one felt for a lost relationship.

She needed Spencer, Isabel realized at the end of the day when they all sat around, talking about ideas for an album name. He made her songs better and when his voice intertwined with hers, it gave her music a completeness that hadn't been there before. *What on earth am I going to do?* Isabel thought, shaking her head.

She prayed for divine intervention.

"So, I think we can call it a night early," Thomas said, and she realized she hadn't been paying attention. Everyone started getting up, chattering, packing up instruments, putting coats on. Isabel lingered at the piano, where she'd been sitting.

"Why don't we all go do something fun for your birthday?" Renee asked Spencer. He told her thanks, but that his uncle was taking him to an old steakhouse they used to eat at a lot when he was younger.

"Think he's got a surprise party in store," he said with a wink. "Wouldn't be surprised if they all made me get up on stage like they did last year."

"You're driving eighty miles all the way out to his ranch now, only to turn around and come back tomorrow?" Thomas asked, without looking up from paper he was examining.

"My birthday," Spencer said. "Can spend it however I want."

Everyone was silent a minute as the two men stared at one another, an air of tension replacing the earlier laughter.

"Well, happy birthday," Renee said, waving.

"Yeah, happy birthday, man," Greg said.

Spencer thanked them as he shrugged on his jacket.

"See you tomorrow," Isabel said. "Happy birthday."

"You too," he whispered, touching her arm a second with one finger as he left.

He and Thomas greeted each other in name only as he left.

When the door shut behind him, Thomas finally spoke to her. "It's your birthday, too?"

Isabel looked up from the piano. *Oh no*. She couldn't say anything.

"How is it that he knows and I don't? Why didn't you tell me?"

Isabel stood up. "I—" she began. "I think Ben may have told him in passing or something. It's no big deal."

"Yeah, right," Thomas scoffed, putting his things in his bag forcefully now.

"Speaking of questions," Isabel said, pushing her hair over her shoulder. "Why did you tell me he and Anna were making out in the lounge if they weren't?"

Thomas stopped what he was doing and looked at her. He didn't have a deer in headlights look, but was staring her down nonetheless.

She kept eye contact. She may have been shy when it came to speaking her mind, but she could stare pretty well. She could stare all night if that's what Thomas wanted.

"Coming down on me, huh?" he asked, tossing his bag on the floor and crossing the room slowly.

Isabel could feel her body falter a bit. No one was there except them.

"Who told you they weren't?" he continued, still walking toward her.

He still hadn't answered her question, she thought. Just returned hers with his own. Well, two could play.

"Does it matter?" she asked.

Thomas stopped right in front of her. "Did you talk to him today?" he asked, searching her face.

Oh, jeez, we're getting nowhere! Isabel rolled her eyes. "It was Renee," she said, crossing her arms. "I ran into her today. The subject came up."

"Oh, so you were checking up on me? Seeing if I was lying?"

Isabel shook her head and grimaced at him, confused. When did he all of a sudden become a victim? "No," she said, falling into defense mode. "Like I said, the subject just came up."

It was Thomas's turn to cross his arms. "Well, I

guess you can believe her or believe me—your boy-friend—whatever you feel is best."

Isabel placed her hands on her temples. All she felt was confusion, and a lot of unneeded drama at the moment.

"Hey," he said, a little softer now. He placed his hands on her arms and she looked up at him. "Why don't you let me take you out for your birthday, and we can just forget about this?"

Isabel looked at him, her hands still on either side of her face but no longer touching it. She didn't really want to go out, and even if she had, she wasn't sure she wanted to go out with Thomas. He still hadn't answered her question.

"I—" She shook her head, gathering her thoughts. "I don't know. Kat's taking me out for dinner."

"Well we could go somewhere after," he said.

"Thomas," she began, holding her hands up, but he interrupted her.

"Hey, meet me at Dale's pub around, say, nine," he said, referencing the little Irish bar on the corner of the square. Isabel knew the place, though she'd never been in. Its sign had a neon green clover that glowed all through the night.

"I don't know," she said again, but Thomas waved her off, gathering up his bag and the rest of his things.

"No, it'll be fun," he insisted. "We can relax, have some drinks, dance—"

"I don't drink much," Isabel said.

"Okay, dessert, then. It'll be a nice little celebration, just you and me."

With that, he threw his bag over his shoulder, came over, and kissed her so forcefully that her head was knocked back a few inches.

Isabel gathered up her stuff and let him walk her out. She still didn't feel great about going out with Thomas as she made her way up to her apartment to get ready, but over dinner at the Blue Ocean, Kat told her that maybe it was his way of apologizing.

"Some men aren't very good at it, you know," Kat said. "My second husband, Vance, certainly wasn't."

"Yeah," Isabel said, rubbing her chin and looking at the wall waterfall near the front of the restaurant. Spencer had, she couldn't help thinking, then told herself to stop. Maybe Kat was right. Maybe this was Thomas's way of apologizing. They hadn't been seeing one another long enough for her to know how he was about these things.

"Kat," Isabel said, laying both hands on either side of her plate.

Kat raised her eyebrows.

"I thought about Spencer when you said that. I thought about him because he apologized to me for Anna."

Isabel told her cousin everything that had happened that day, from his and Renee's explanations to his birthday gift for her, to the song they did, to her thoughts about him. Kat just watched her as she explained all of this.

"I think about him all the time, Kat!" she exclaimed. "He's everywhere, he's in everything. And I'm supposed to be dating his friend?"

Kat took a sip of her tea and set it on the table before her. She took a long and deep breath and laced her fingers together before her on the table.

Isabel laughed, running her hands through her hair. "I don't know what to do, Kat. I don't know what to do."

Kat reached forward and poked Isabel's arm, bringing her back. Her answer was simple. "I think, actually, that you know exactly what to do."

♫♫♫

By the time Isabel got back to her apartment she only had five minutes to freshen up before meeting Thomas. She rushed around her apartment, reapplying lipstick, brushing her hair. She was so nervous, she had to reapply deodorant twice. In a way, though, she was glad for the lack of time. Too much time meant too much thinking, questioning, second-guessing. She knew what she needed to do. It was time to stop jerking Thomas around. He needed to know how she felt. And the sooner she told him, the sooner he could find someone he deserved, someone who felt the same about him as he did about her.

Isabel almost twisted her ankle skipping down the stairs and nearly knocked a couple over as she threw the door of her building open. She apologized over her shoulder as she ran down the street toward the lighted shamrock. It was already five after nine when she pulled open the heavy glass door and walked into the bar and showed her ID to a burly guy at the front with a long red beard. He waved her in, wished her a happy birthday and she smiled at him.

Isabel had never been inside Dale's before. It was a narrow restaurant with a laminate wood bar stretching from nearly the front of the place all the way to the back and a wall-to-wall mirror behind it. Right across from that were creaky wooden booths. A blue neon sign near the back said "Pool Room." It was pretty packed, so Isabel had a seat at the bar near the door.

A tall, slim bartender with floppy dark hair and sleeves of his button-up shirt rolled up sauntered over and tossed a napkin in front of her, asked her what she'd have. Isabel opened her mouth to protest at first, but then thought, *What the hell?* It was her birthday, after all. She ordered an Amaretto Sour. When he brought it back, she described Thomas, asked if he'd seen him.

"Nope, no one in here like that," he said, taking the five dollar bill she set on the counter. She told him to keep the change. She took her cell out and checked it for messages but there was nothing. It was now ten after nine.

Probably just running late, she thought, taking sip of her drink. It was hot as it ran down inside of her and she had to let out a breath. When she looked up, she saw the bartender catch her eye, smile at her. She looked away, but couldn't help smiling back before she did. She looked up at the television in the corner. It was showing some soccer game. It took her all of five minutes of watching that before she turned back to cell again. Nine-fifteen. Isabel found Thomas's number and hit "send." It went straight to voicemail. Every time the door opened, she turned, expecting to see him arrive, but each time it was a dressed-up couple, a small group of twenty-somethings, and an older man who didn't even have to show his ID. She tried calling him again at nine-thirty and then again at nine-forty. She tried calling Renee to see if she'd heard from him.

"No, I haven't heard anything," Renee said, her tone just slightly close to worried.

"I'm sure he's just running late," Isabel said, trying to bring her back. She regretted calling, now, because it seemed like Renee was going to worry. She hung up and saw Spencer's number just below Renee's in her phone and thought about hitting it, but stopped herself. If she called Spencer, it wouldn't be because she was looking for Thomas and she knew it. Besides, he was out of town.

At nine-forty-five, a certainty began to sink in and she found herself staring at the mirror without really seeing herself.

The bartender came over and asked if she needed anything else. Isabel couldn't do much more than shake her head. Her voice was too quiet to be heard amidst the sounds of people talking and shouting and some Irish folk song echoing from the speakers. Finally, a little after ten, she pulled her coat back over her shoulders and stepped outside into the freezing, damp night air.

Despite the noise from inside, it was quiet out there on the street. Not even a lone car passed by. Isabel pushed her hands in her pockets and looked all around. Not a soul except hers occupied the street. She looked at the buildings surrounding the courthouse. A few lights burned in the upstairs of each, along with the ever-lit trees around.

People were inside, with others or alone, reading, watching television, sleeping. But she wasn't. She was alone. That was how it felt, being stood up, she realized. Alone, small. She took a last look around. The buildings seemed so much larger at night when no one was around. Funny, Isabel thought. She'd never noticed it before now.

♫♫♫

Eighty miles away, Spencer sat against the wall in the back booth of Smitty's Tavern. It was only a little after ten, but between the drive straight there, spending most of the evening talking with old friends and family he hadn't seen in year, people his introverted Uncle Jack had taken time to round up for this impromptu surprise party he'd planned, and then singing and playing guitar an hour straight up there on stage, he was beat. He sat back, took a drink of his whiskey and closed his eyes just to relax a minute.

If he headed back to Jack's—who'd left an hour ago—he'd be able to get about six hours' sleep before he had to be on the road again the next morning to make it back to the studio.

He tried to be grateful for this party and all of these people, but right now, finally being able to take a moment for himself, he thought about how there was really only one person he wanted to spend his birthday with, and that was Isabel. Or maybe just the birthday night, he admitted to himself as he took another drink. He couldn't help smiling as he thought about what *that* might be like. And then there was the way they could talk about anything, especially that first day in the bookstore and on the town square.

They hadn't had a chance much lately like that first day, but that was still there as evidenced by their conversation today. And, of course, there were also the little moments. The way she'd look over at him when she sang and how they'd just look at each other, just look, but for a second too long. The way she'd laugh at herself and her music, embarrassed and still not knowing how good she was, even after all these weeks. The sweet way she widened her eyes, surprised by his birthday gift. The way she hugged him, let him hold her back.

No, he thought, moving his head down to rest his chin on his elbow on the table. It wasn't just physical although that was definitely a part of it.

She's dating your friend, the little voice of reason snapped at him from within.

And it's driving me crazy, he snapped back. It was, too. Not being able to look at her, talk to her the way he wanted. Not being able to take her hand, give her a simple hug, or, what he'd been thinking about most, kiss her. He couldn't do any of that. And he got to watch Thomas do it day in and day out.

Spencer groaned a low growl, exasperated, and scratched the back of his head.

"Something botherin' you, tiger?" said a familiar voice, seemingly coming from miles away.

Spencer opened his eyes and saw one of his high school girlfriends, Maggie, standing inches away from his booth. She looked great—long dark hair sleek as it had ever been, eyes bright and green. Despite the cold outside, she wore skintight jeans and an equally tight camisole. A turquoise pendant dangled precariously low past her neckline, exactly where she was trying to draw attention, if he remembered her correctly. Judging from her smile and the way she ran her tongue over her upper lip, just slightly so as not to take away the fire-red lipstick, Spencer supposed he was right.

"Maggie," he said, sitting up, gesturing across from him for her to have a seat. She did, sighing just loudly enough to be audible, to draw his eyes to hers.

"You did great tonight," she said, nodding toward the stage.

"Could've joined me," he said, taking another drink of his whiskey.

Almost to the bottom. A couple of more sips, it'd be gone. It's not like she hadn't joined him onstage before. The girl couldn't carry a tune in a bucket, but still, he used to reach out, pull her on stage with him all the time when he performed in this bar some twelve years ago. She was never afraid to do anything. She was the only girl in high school who would hop onto the back of his motorcycle and tell him to go, just go.

One morning in May, close to graduation and eternal freedom from school, they did just that, flying along the back country roads, nothing but wind and wildness all around, ditching school and her bag still sitting on the ground.

They didn't need a bag to do what they'd done that day, anyway.

Spencer half laughed to himself.

"What's so funny?" she asked, leaning forward over the table so that her shirt inched the slightest bit lower.

"Thinking about that time we ditched school that day, just took off on my bike."

"Hmm," she said, returning his smile. "I remember.

That was probably one of the best days of my life."

"Why?" he asked, looking at her. He took another small sip, making his whiskey last.

Maggie smiled, bit her lip a second before answering, "You really have to ask?"

They held one another's gazes for a second. No, he didn't.

"Anyway, it was fun, wasn't it?" she continued. "Not having to worry about anything—school, jobs, anyone telling us what to do. Freedom. That should be my name. Freedom. I love it, don't you?"

She said it slowly the last time, touched her pendant with manicured nails.

"It was fun," he conceded, though not answering her question. He ran a finger along the rim of his glass. "A last good time before real life kicked in."

And it had been fun, too. Like she said. Nothing—no one—to worry about. Just them, just fun.

"How long are you here for?" she asked.

"Leave tomorrow morning," he said.

"So soon," she pretended to pout. "Was hoping we could spend a little time together."

He shrugged. "Sorry. Don't know what to tell you."

He started to bring the whiskey glass to his mouth to take that last sip when Maggie reached up, placed her fingertips on his hand that was holding the glass, a crackle of fire just under her touch. She kept eye contact and smiled the whole time she took the glass from him, brought it to her own mouth and finished his drink.

"You look sad," she said, setting the empty glass before her. Then she made her move. "I have an idea. Why don't you take this little bit of time you're going to still be in town, come back to my house with me and—"

He didn't say anything. So, she continued.

"And you don't have to *tell* me anything. As a matter of fact, what I have in mind doesn't involve talking at all. We don't have to say anything, worry about anything or anyone. For tonight, it'll just be fun, just like before."

Spencer looked at her a long moment. He should just leave. Just go back to Laurel Springs. There was no point in staying, no point in spending the night with her. He reached into his pocket, and pulled out some cash to leave on the table. He left his waitress a good tip, moved out of the booth, and took his time putting his coat on.

Maggie still sat, looking at him with those electric green eyes. He stood staring at her another moment before holding out his hand, which she took with a smile.

They said nothing, not another word, as they drove back to her house, entered her darkened bedroom, joined together in her bed. They drifted from sex to sleep in silence.

Maggie said nothing, demanded nothing, and remained sleeping as the stars and moon still glowed in the cold November sky, and Spencer, like a departing ghost, quietly dressed, locked her door behind him, and began the drive back to Laurel Springs.

♫ ♫ ♫

Isabel stayed up half the night, feeling pitiful and sorry for herself. She tried turning on an episode of *Andy Griffith* because it always comforted and relaxed her to sleep, but it turned out to be the episode where Andy and his girlfriend, Peggy, keep missing meeting each other for dates and she ends up thinking he stood her up. Isabel rolled her eyes, turned over, and pulled the comforter over her head.

She didn't know when she'd finally fallen asleep or how long she stayed asleep, but when she pulled the cover off of her head and looked at the clock at nine the next morning, she felt like it hadn't been that long. The migraine pounding the right side of her head probably had a lot to do with it. She drank a bottle of water, had three Ibuprofens and a cup of coffee before checking her phone again and finding that she had no missed calls, not from Thomas, not from anyone.

That was fine. The way she felt, she didn't want to talk to Thomas right now. She ran the shower in the bathroom and stepped in, letting the hot water run over her face and body. She didn't even know what she felt right then.

Part of her was confused. Had he known what she was going to say to him that evening and that's why he didn't show? She was also still just a little worried. Was something wrong? Wouldn't someone have gotten in touch with her by now if there was? And then there was the part of her that was angry as hell at him for leaving her there like that in that bar, all alone. Where the hell was he? Why hadn't he even called her? Isabel dried herself off with a clean towel and blew her hair dry, dressed in jeans and a blue turtleneck. She stood there putting on her makeup, wondering how she was going to be able to go in there and work with him if she couldn't get some kind of explanation from him first.

She took her phone out as she as she grabbed her coat and her bag. He didn't seem like the type to just stand her or anyone up. She pulled out her phone and scrolled through her contacts until she found his name as she closed the door to the stairwell behind her and tapped it when she got to it.

It started ringing just as she passed the window of the coffee shop below her loft. But what she saw—who she saw—beyond that window, made her stop. Thomas was there, right there, at the counter, taking a cup of coffee from the barista with one hand and his ringing phone out of his pocket with his other.

Isabel stood motionless as she watched him take his phone out, look at it a split second, hit a button, and replace it in his pocket.

The next thing Isabel saw as she was accosted with the sound of his outgoing message on his voice mail, was the image of him taking the coffee to a woman sitting at one of the tables on the other side of the shop, a woman with a shock of short blonde hair.

And then he kissed her, just once.

Chapter 12

December 12, 2016:

Almost immediately upon entering the studio, Isabel was approached by a tall but young red-headed woman wearing dark red lipstick and a black suit. The woman was on a cell phone in the front room to the right of the main stairwell, but when she saw Isabel, she immediately said to the other person on the line, "I'll call you right back!"

She ran over, holding out her manicured hand.

"Ms. Carson, so nice to finally meet you. How are you?" she asked, jerking Isabel's hand up and down.

Isabel removed her soft pink wool hat and opened

her mouth, but the redhead didn't give her a chance to answer.

"I'm Hope Weston, the new manager for Shiloh Ridge. I'm so happy you could make it for this reunion."

She put her hand on Isabel's back and pushed her forward into the front room that looked exactly the same as it had eight years ago—wooden floors and paneling on the walls, windows lining the far wall letting in the late morning sun.

The people inside looked just a bit different, though. There were a couple of guys, a lean one with blond hair longer than her own and another taller one with hard brown eyes and a button-up shirt over his broad shoulders, talking with Greg and Renee, each of whom wore wedding bands now. Greg was taller somehow, not quite as heavy, but had some gray at the temples, and Renee wore her hair short and layered, parted mostly to one side. She was listening to something Hard Eyes was saying until Hope cleared her throat. "Everyone?"

Renee was the first to look her way. Her eyes lit up when she saw Isabel, and she came over right away and threw her arms around her friend. "Isabel!" she screamed. "How've you been? What have you been up to? *Where* have you been all this time? You look great! I can't believe you're finally back here!"

Isabel had to laugh at Renee's questions. "I'm good," she said nodding. "You look wonderful. I'm so happy to see you."

And it was the truth, about Renee, anyway. Hope's cell buzzed and she thrust it at her ear and immediately began shouting at the person on the other end and gesturing with her other hand. She walked to the other end of the room near the windows while Renee kept peppering Isabel with comments and questions. Isabel just laughed again as she fiddled with her hat and her coffee and looked at the floor, barely having a chance to answer.

When she looked up again, her eyes landed right on Thomas, who was walking toward her and that's when all of her relaxation gave way to paralysis. She had to consciously force herself to bring her hand forward, shake his when he offered.

"Thank you for coming," was all he said.

At first glance, he looked exactly the same, but as she looked at him a beat longer, Isabel could see the lines forming around his mouth and his blue eyes that were even icier than the last time she'd seem them.

"Thomas," she returned in greeting.

She couldn't muster anything other than a small nod and had to look away, back at Renee's smiling, welcoming, safe face. Greg greeted her with a half-hug and Renee introduced her to Jason, the blond guy who didn't smile, but reached forward and immediately shook hands and nodded in greeting, and Jacob, whose eyes softened as he greeted her, but whose face otherwise kept a stony stare. He reminded Isabel of statues she'd seen of Zeus, only younger.

"Well, I think this is everyone," Hope said as she ended her call, making another grand gesture toward everyone.

Is it? Isabel thought, looking around.

As if reading her mind, Hope looked all around her. "Hey, where did Mr. Logan go?"

Right then, Spencer came around the corner, half-waved to everyone with two fingers.

"Right here," he said.

Isabel had to touch the wall behind her to steady herself. He, too, had just a few more lines on his face, and his hair was shorter. But it was still a thick, shaggy mess and his eyes still carried the same blue flame she'd fallen for years ago. And damn it, could he fill out that leather jacket and jeans.

Isabel closed her eyes a second but instead of tears coming to her eyes, she half-smiled, half-laughed inside at herself. After all this time, everything that had happened between them and after, he could still do that to her.

She had just turned her eyes to the window when he said to her in greeting, "Isabel."

She turned her eyes back. He was looking at her, just looking, keeping his distance. "Hi," she said in return. Her voice had barely made a sound.

"So, what I was thinking," Hope said, bringing everyone's eyes and attention back to her. "Is that today you would all focus on reacquainting yourselves and gathering your bearings, maybe talk about or pitch songs you'd like to see on this next album. Then tomorrow we will start rehearsals and interviews..."

"Interviews?" Isabel whispered to Renee.

Renee turned her head slightly. "Yeah, this woman has a whole production planned. Has newspaper and magazine reporters coming in to spend about five minutes here and there with each of us, then some with all of us, collectively."

Renee giggled, but Isabel couldn't return it. Interviews are not exactly what she'd signed up for, though she was hardly surprised. The more publicity, the more chance of success. She looked at the floor, trying to listen to Hope's words about the upcoming concert but could hardly register them. When she looked up again, her eyes landed on Spencer across the way. He'd been watching her, she realized. He smiled a little when her eyes met his, then looked down and away. Isabel couldn't smile back.

When Hope finished her spiel, she said she would leave all of them to it and left, still looking at her phone. She said she'd be in and out of her hotel all day but recited her cell phone number, told everyone to program it into their own, just in case they needed to reach her. She could hear Thomas suggesting to everyone a Mexican restaurant for dinner.

Isabel knew the place. It was loud and colorful, decorated in turquoise and coral with bright lights, Mariachi band music and the shuffle of shoes and chairs across the terra-cotta floor, a place they could hardly talk. Everyone agreed that was the best place. Thomas said half an hour. Isabel had just turned away from the crowd, still trying program Hope's number into her phone when she heard, "Can I talk to you a minute?"

She looked up to see Thomas's icy eyes appraising her face. Her first instinct was to say no. She didn't want to be alone with him, especially after the last time they'd been alone, and especially now, after they hadn't seen one another in years. But then, as she thought about that last time they'd seen one another, the last things they'd said and done, she couldn't help but think that whatever he had to say now had to be good.

Isabel shrugged her indifference.

"The roof?" he suggested.

She nodded. "Okay."

It was only when he turned away that she could feel her heart pounding. He'd approached her so suddenly that she hadn't even noticed it before. She let him go first, took her time programming Hope's number into her phone.

When she looked up again, she saw Spencer across the room, backlit by the late afternoon sun. He didn't look away when she looked up at him. It was hard to see his face, being silhouetted by the sun the way he was, but she felt she caught a glimmer of a smile, an invitation that reminded her of the night they met. He remained relaxed as he took a small step toward her. It was nothing more, but it made Isabel jump, sent her walking toward the stairs. She didn't make it up the first step. She held onto the bannister, looking at that first step. She couldn't walk past it.

It wasn't a matter of whether or not she wanted to. It was the image she saw of herself, lying at the bottom of that stairway, clutching her side, feeling an internal pain she had never felt before that, and never again after. She stumbled backward a few steps, landing against a strong pair of hands that felt all too familiar. She twisted around to look into Spencer's concerned fire-blue eyes.

"You okay?" he asked, his voice almost a whisper.

She could hear the velvet night sky in his voice again and was suddenly angry. Where was that voice, those hands, six years ago? She shook her head, pulled out of his grip, wondering if it even mattered anymore at this point.

"I'm fine," she snapped.

She couldn't walk out onto the sidewalk fast enough. She dug her hand in her jeans pocket, retrieved her phone and found the number that Thomas had called her from all those days ago.

"If you want to talk to me, you can do it out here in front of the building," she said when she heard him answer.

She didn't give him a chance to respond before hitting the "End" button and having a seat on the bench just in front of one the crepe myrtles. She sat on one end, close to the edge, her arms wrapped around her.

Despite her coat and hat, the cold almost instantly settled in past her skin and all the way down to her bones. But she still didn't know if it was that or nerves making her shiver.

Chapter 13

November 11, 2009:

Isabel!"

Isabel hadn't heard the banging on her door, but she certainly heard the sound of Thomas yelling her name. She groaned, pulling the covers back over her head. When she'd seen Thomas kiss that woman, she'd run straight through town square, ignoring cars honking at her, not stopping until she got clear on the other side, already sweating through her turtleneck. She'd looked all around, seeing nothing but white haze and confusion. Thomas was cheating on her? With who? Jessie? Was that Jessie?

When she'd calmed down enough to see clearly and focus, she'd almost laughed at the irony that she'd been sitting there, harboring feelings for Thomas's friend, and here he was, seeing someone else behind her back. She saw she was in front of George Carter's bookstore and had gone in to sink into one of the deep armchairs and think. The Ibuprofen she'd taken had worn off almost immediately and her migraine returned with a vengeance. She didn't want to go to the studio, anyway, so she called Kat and told her, so she wouldn't worry, then went home, gobbled more Ibuprofen, and collapsed in bed. She raised her head and reached for her phone to see what time it was.

Now he was banging on her door again. "Isabel!"

She didn't answer. She didn't want to see Thomas, and she certainly didn't want to talk to him.

"Isabel, I need to talk to you! Please, just give me a chance to explain!"

Isabel rolled her eyes beneath the covers. Explain? Well, that should be good.

She turned over and tried to roll out of bed and landed on the floor.

"Ugh," she said, bringing a hand to her throbbing head. More banging. More calls from Thomas.

"I heard you in there, I know you're home!"

"Just a minute!" she finally yelled back, her hands on her temples. She never should've gotten out of bed that morning. She sighed, rubbing her eyes and stumbling to the door. He didn't ask for an invitation when she opened the door, just walked right in. "I didn't invite you in," she mumbled, rubbing her forehead.

"What?"

She shook her head, waving him off. "What do you want?"

"Honey, you didn't show up at the studio, I was worried."

Isabel raised her eyebrows as she tried to focus her eyes beyond the blur that was her vision. "I have a migraine. And are you seriously lecturing me on showing up to things?"

"Isabel," he said, starting again. His face was eager, his eyes wide, like he'd been looking a lifetime for her. She folded her arms and leaned against her kitchen counter. Here it was. This should be good. "My dad's in the hospital," he said. His voice was rushed, sounding worried.

Isabel perked up, could feel her body and brain focus just a little more. She looked at the floor. Was that even true?

"He was in a car accident, just a fender bender, but they brought him in to the hospital and kept him for observation because of his age. I couldn't leave him or my mom. She was a nervous wreck."

Isabel stared at him a long moment, the image of him and Jessie still at the forefront of her mind. "Is this true?" she asked.

Thomas nodded, not saying anything more for now. Okay, she would play along. Maybe this was true.

"I'm sorry. Is he okay?"

Thomas nodded again, a look of eager relief passing over his face.

"Yeah, thanks, yeah. He'll be coming home later to-day."

He was only sporadically making eye contact with her. He smiled and half-laughed as he ran a hand through his hair. Isabel just watched him.

"So, um, I guess we'd better get to work," he said, jerking his thumb in the direction of her front door.

"I guess we should," Isabel said. She didn't move. Thomas grimaced.

"You feel okay? If you don't—"

"You must have been so worried about your dad," she interrupted.

"Uh, yeah, I was. Yeah." Thomas shifted around, put his hands in his pockets.

"I guess that's why you weren't able to answer my calls last night. And this morning."

Thomas cocked his head to the side, a sheepish look on his face.

"Yeah, about that, I was thinking we could go out tonight. I'll pick you up after I check on dad, take you to dinner."

"Maybe I could just go with you to see him. Give me a chance to meet your parents."

Thomas shook his head, looking at the ground again. Again, he laughed.

"He should probably rest. Probably shouldn't endure the stress of meeting someone new."

"Sorry, didn't know I was stressful."

"Oh, no, I didn't mean it like that."

"I know. Just kidding."

They stood staring at one another a moment longer.

"Well," Isabel finally said. "If there's nothing else, I guess we really should get back to work on that last song."

"You're okay, right?" Thomas asked, the edge of worry back in his voice. "I mean, you understand, right? Why I couldn't be there?"

"I do," Isabel said, smiling evenly. "There is just one other thing, though."

Thomas waited.

"Who was that woman you were with at the coffee shop this morning? The one with short blonde hair that you gave coffee to and kissed. Was she there with you when you heard about your dad?"

Thomas didn't miss a beat. He grimaced and widened his eyes. "What are you talking about?"

"I'm talking about when I called you and you ignored my call and took that woman coffee and then kissed her."

"What? I don't know what you saw, Isabel, but I wasn't there this morning. I was with my dad."

"Thomas," Isabel said. She could feel her heart picking up speed, her face flushing. She hated being lied to worse than anything. "I know what you look like. You were wearing that very coat you're still wearing."

Isabel pointed out the brown coat she'd seen from outside the coffee shop. Thomas, for the first time that day, was speechless. He shrugged.

"I don't know what you want me to say," he said.

"Was that Jessie?" Isabel asked, ignoring his statement.

He opened his mouth to answer and Isabel held up her hand, shaking her head. She'd changed her mind.

"You know what? Never mind. It doesn't matter." And it didn't.

"Well, I want to explain. Please, hear me out. Let me tell you what happened."

He was closing the distance between them, his hands held out as if giving her an offering of some kind. She wanted none of it. Not only had he lied, he'd cheated, too.

"Thomas," Isabel began, turning around and putting a hand on her hip. "It's fine. All of it. It's fine."

He froze where he was. "Why?" he demanded, his tone darkening.

Isabel could feel tension rise at the darker sound in his voice, like he wasn't about to let her say what she was going to say. "Because I think we should just call it quits, anyway. I was planning on telling you that last night." It was her turn to get her words out fast.

"Why?" he said again, moving closer toward her. He wasn't as tall as Spencer, but he was pretty menacing when he got that close with that shadow over his eyes. Isabel took an instinctive step back.

"Thomas," she began.

He seemed to snap out of it. He shook his head, half-laughed.

"I'm sorry," he said for the first time. Then, "Please. Just let me explain. She called me and yeah, I did see her—"

"There's nothing to explain." Isabel felt calmer now, could hear it in her voice. "If you want her, then that's okay."

"But why is it okay? Why are you so okay with just ending our relationship?"

"I guess for the same reason you were okay with cheating on me with your ex," Isabel said, her voice rising. She knew her words were true. Though she hadn't technically physically cheated on Thomas, she may as well have in her mind—and with his friend, no less.

Thomas grimaced at her for a moment before a realization passed over his eyes. "You're seeing someone else, too, aren't you?"

"I haven't been," she said. "But to be honest, there is someone else, someone—"

"Who?" Thomas yelled, getting in her face.

"That's really none of your business."

"Isabel," he said, getting closer to her. "Tell me who it is."

"Thomas—"

"Right now!"

"Okay, you know what?" Isabel straightened. He was not going to do this to her. "You need to leave. Right now."

She hoped she sounded as authoritative as she tried to be, hoped he wouldn't see the fear he'd brought upon her or hear the shake in her voice. He didn't give any indication either way. He stood glaring at her and she at him until she moved around him to go open the door.

Thomas turned around but didn't make a move to leave just yet.

"Do that last song without me," she said, looking out into the hallway. "You're almost done with it. You don't need me so much on it, anyway."

Thomas took slow, heavy steps toward the door. He stopped right in front of her, towering over her. She didn't look up.

"Fine, Isabel," he said. There was no affection or kindness when he used her name now.

"Tour bus leaves for Myrtle Beach next week," he said in a low tone. "Thursday, noon. We leave from the studio. I expect you to be on it and to not miss any more rehearsals, recording sessions, or any concerts for that matter. Do you understand?"

His tone was authoritative. It was clear he wasn't

talking to his girlfriend anymore. He was talking to his employee, one he didn't think much of. He'd never been her lover, and he was certainly no longer her boyfriend.

"I understand," Isabel said, turning her eyes up to glare at him.

"One last thing," he said.

Isabel waited.

"This other person you're seeing or thinking about or whatever."

She kept her eyes on his.

"It damn well better not be Spencer."

Isabel turned her head up just a little more. She wanted to ask him why not, what was wrong with Spencer. She knew the story he told her of Spencer being a ladies' man, but something else, something in his eyes told her there was more to that story. So, she stood there, as she and Thomas stared one another down, and she didn't ask why not, because then he would know that it was, in fact, Spencer, his band mate, his friend, that she had feelings for.

He walked out without saying good bye. Isabel locked the door immediately behind him and slid to the floor. She didn't realize how fast her heart was pounding until after he left.

Chapter 14

December 12, 2016:

It only took a few seconds before the door was thrown open and Thomas appeared, his hands out in front of him in question.

"What's up?" he asked.

Isabel scowled in his general direction. "I can't go up those stairs."

She looked at the crepe myrtle before her, its branches bare in the winter air except for the twinkle lights that wrapped around it. They'd be on soon when the darkness fell. Very soon.

Thomas sat down, not too close to her. "Fine," he

said, not bothering with an apology. "There's only one thing I have to say to you, anyway."

Isabel studied the branches on the crepe myrtle before her. She had a good feeling what that one thing was.

"I want to make sure you and Spencer can get through this without getting into each other's pants."

Isabel's mouth dropped open and she looked at him, disgusted. "Ex*cu*se me?" she asked. She couldn't believe he had the nerve to put it that way.

"It's rude and disrespectful, especially to me."

"What are you *talking* about?"

"Well, what can I say? Except some wounds never really heal."

Isabel couldn't move, couldn't talk for a moment after he said that. She felt something rising in her chest, a catch, a balloon, keeping her from finding her words. She started and then stopped a couple of times before she finally just swallowed, but as Thomas stood up to leave, his point made, she finally did uncover exactly what she needed to say.

"And what about what you did to me?" she asked, her voice low but nonetheless detectable.

Thomas turned around but didn't say anything.

Isabel swallowed once before standing and continuing, "Don't you think that the wound you gave me was enough?"

Enough to keep you from dictating what I do and don't do. Not that she could hardly even look at Spencer.

After all, he'd hurt her almost as much as Thomas had. Almost.

And yet he still didn't know the whole story, Isabel reminded herself. She held him accountable, and he didn't even know what had happened the night he'd left her shell-shocked and alone in the studio that night, taking his victory and his triumph. She blamed him, but still just couldn't tell him why.

"Look," he said when she didn't continue. "I know we're all going to be spending a lot of time together these next few months, maybe even longer. And we all need to be at our best because we really need this album to be good."

Especially after the last one you released, Isabel couldn't help thinking.

"So there doesn't need to be any awkwardness. Do you understand?"

Isabel grimaced. Had he really just spoken to her like she was a five-year-old? She blinked once, nodded.

"Good," he said, nodding once as well and turning to look at his reflection in the glass. He ran a hand through his hair, made sure he looked cool. "Can't wait to hear what you've been working on these past few years."

He didn't look at her again as he opened the door and entered the building, leaving her out there on the street.

Isabel could feel the balloon in her chest again, and struggled against it to breathe. She replayed his words from minutes before, and then heard the ones he'd said to her years before, just before she slipped, fell, and landed like a rag doll at the bottom of the stairs. She saw and heard and felt Spencer from moments ago, then from years ago, the night they met, when it was just the two of them. It felt like stars colliding.

All of her thoughts started spinning in circles, like the contents in a witch's pot and she couldn't see, couldn't hear, couldn't think. The door of the studio opened. She turned away, took off. She didn't run, but walked fast, with purpose, like she knew where she was going. She had to get out of there. She could hear the footsteps behind her, following her. But she didn't turn around and wasn't scared, like another woman alone on the edge of darkness might be. She had an idea of who it was, there, following her, not speaking to her but calling for her nonetheless with his fast footsteps. He was taller, his legs longer, and he just might catch up to her if she didn't make to the stoplight to cross the street first. She could see in the distance the little lighted *DON'T WALK* sign, but knew she still had a couple of seconds before the streetlights turned green. If she made it, she could cross and lose him before—

She felt a hand close underneath her bicep, and she yanked it away before he could get a grip. Almost to the end of the road. Two cars were waiting. Their drivers weren't looking at her, but at the stoplight before them, seconds away from turning green. She still had time.

A millisecond before she stepped onto the crosswalk,

though, he grabbed her arm again, this time not losing his grip as she tried to pull it away. Both cars pushed forward, her chance gone with them. She fought against his strong arms and hands, hitting at him and pushing away as he almost effortlessly pulled her into a small darkened alley between two buildings behind one of the crepe myrtles whose lights were already gleaming.

"Get off," she hissed.

But he didn't. He pulled her face to his and kissed her violently, still holding her with his other arm.

Chapter 15

November 2009:

The tour bus was a large black and white affair with red trim along the sides. Isabel was the first one there and actually found the door to it open, so she decided to go on in and get acquainted with it and everything. It was pretty spacious, with everything they'd need for an overnight trip. Most of the seats near the front and the sectional surrounding a small kitchen table were brown leather.

There were six bunk beds near the back with little curtains to shut out noise and light, a bathroom with an actual shower, a kitchen area with a microwave, mini-fridge and coffeepot across from the sitting area which held two couches and two seats across from each other and a television bolted into the corner.

"Wow," she said, placing her duffel bag on the top right bunk. This was almost the size of her little loft.

"What's that?" she heard an unfamiliar voice say from behind. Isabel jumped and turned around to find a middle-aged man with salt and pepper hair and about ten pounds of extra weight around his mid-section.

"Hey there, I'm Mike," he said, holding out his hand and shaking her hand vigorously.

Isabel smiled and introduced herself.

"Good to meet you. I'll be getting you all to where you're going over the next few months. You need anything, want to stop anywhere, I'm your man."

He jerked his thumb at his own chest and Isabel laughed and thanked him. She couldn't imagine anyone else driving this house on wheels.

Renee and Greg were the next to arrive.

"Isabel, hey!" Renee said, practically getting right up in Isabel's face after she and Greg has stored their bags on their bunks. "You all right?" she asked, though it seemed more like a demand.

"I am." Isabel nodded, and it was the truth. It had been several days since she and Thomas had broken up and each day actually got a little easier.

"Um," Renee said, looking behind her where Greg was just walking down the steps of the bus to get everyone some coffee. "I'm not going to butt in, but I did hear about you and Thomas."

Isabel looked at the ground and tried to smile, but it came forth awkwardly. "Uh," she began.

"I'm not going to ask what happened. That's between y'all, but I just wanted you to know that if you want to talk, I'm here, okay?"

"Thomas didn't tell you anything?"

Renee shook her head. "Just said that you guys weren't compatible."

Isabel raised her eyebrows and had to nod. Well, he was right about that. She wasn't compatible with someone who could lie and cheat as easily as he could breathe and eat. Isabel reached out and hugged Renee, who automatically returned the hug. "Thanks," she said.

"For what?" they could hear someone say and turned to see Thomas coming up the steps to the bus, lugging two duffle bags. "Isabel," he said in a monotone greeting. "Renee."

"Hi, Thomas," Isabel said.

"Hi," Renee said.

Thomas stopped and looked at where Isabel had put her bags.

"This is my bunk," he said, taking her bag and shoving it in her direction.

She caught it just before it hit the floor.

"Sorry," she said, putting it on a bunk across the way.

"Spencer here yet?" was his only reply.

"Haven't seen him," said Renee, who watched the scene before her with raised eyebrows.

"He'd better get a move on before we leave his ass on the side of the road. Mike!" he shouted. "Get this bucket of junk started! We need to be in Myrtle Beach before dark! It's after twelve as it is."

He began making his way toward the front.

"Sure thing, Thomas," Mike said, his jolly mood unfazed by Thomas's grouchy one.

Wow, Isabel thought. She never thought she'd be one to bring out the worst in someone. But she thought she might've just accomplished that.

In the end, they didn't leave Spencer behind. He dashed onto the bus minutes before they pulled out, threw his bag onto a random bunk and had a seat in the seating area where they were all talking about the show the next night—or rather, Thomas was doing the talking, telling everyone exactly how he wanted it to go, from what order they'd do what songs, which ones they'd preview from this new album, etc. Spencer didn't sit next to Isabel, instead opting to sit directly across. She could feel him look at her from time to time, but she kept her eyes on her notebook. She didn't know if Thomas had said anything to him about their breakup or what. The only thing she did know was that she wanted to be alone with him.

They arrived in Myrtle Beach a little after six that night, just before the sun set. They checked in at a small motel called the Silver Bay Inn. It was tiny, but clean, and the rooms were quaint with cream carpets, fluffy bed comforters, blue and white tiled bathrooms and photographs of the sea at sunrise and sunset on the walls. Plus, it was right on the beach.

They didn't get much of a chance to enjoy it, though. No sooner had Isabel collapsed on her bed did Thomas bang on her door, telling her it was time to get to the venue. The air was warm and humid and smelled like the sea and felt like the sand, even inland near Broadway where the festival was being held. The amphitheater where most of the bands and entertainment would be playing stood behind rides that glowed neon shades of green, blue, red, and yellow.

A burly man with a white mustache and hair greeted them as they filed out of the bus, shaking hands first with Thomas and Spencer and telling them how good it was to see them again.

"Shiloh Ridge always brings in the most people," he said. "I know it'll be as big a show as last year, maybe bigger."

Isabel felt a small twitch, a flutter inside as he said that. Lots of people, all out there cheering, making noise. Oh, jeez, what if she forgot the music? The words? What if she got them booed off stage? If Thomas hated her now, which, undoubtedly, he did, he certainly would hate her and fire her then. He'd probably leave her right there at the beach.

Oh well, she thought, trying to smile as the burly man introduced himself as Jefferson, told her he was the coordinator for the events at the festival. *At least Kat won't mind coming to get me.*

Isabel swallowed hard and tried to breathe, a feat that was becoming harder as Jefferson led them through a narrow hallway where their dressing rooms were and up the stairs of the amphitheater, smaller than Isabel would have thought, that faced an open field, beyond which were about a million trees.

The drum set was set up near the back of the stage and mics and lights were set up overhead, but other than that, it was cavernous, open. How in the world were they going to fill up that stage? How was this going to work? Isabel could feel her heart start to pound, imagined a thousand people out there, waiting expectantly while she tried to find the words to sing, but couldn't, let alone find a voice.

"Enjoy the carnival if you want, guys," Thomas said, bringing her back to the moment. "We have to be back here for rehearsals at two and then the sound check at four tomorrow. We go on at five."

And with that, he left them all. Renee begged Greg to ride the Ferris wheel with her and he rolled his eyes but laughed and relented. They waved to Spencer and Isabel as they left, telling them they'd see them tomorrow. Isabel waved back before taking her messenger bag off her shoulder and setting it on the stage. She walked the length of it, taking it in, thinking if she just did that, just let it in, then it wouldn't be so bad tomorrow night when she had to get up here in front of all those people and entertain them.

She sighed, taking in the sight of the open field before her that would be packed the following night.

"Quite a sight, isn't it?"

Isabel turned. She hadn't realized Spencer was standing several feet behind her.

"Hey," she said. "Yeah, I was just thinking—about tomorrow night."

"First time's always a little hard," he admitted. "But don't worry, after your first song, you'll be fine."

"You sure?" she asked.

He turned to her and raised an eyebrow slightly and she had to giggle.

"You'll be fine," he assured her again. "You know these songs by heart by now. Plus, we'll all be there. You won't be by yourself."

Isabel took a breath.

"You might just have fun," he said, leaning in close and nudging her shoulder.

Isabel couldn't help but laugh again. She guessed it was nerves.

"I'll help you out if anything happens," Spencer said.

"Yeah, you're quite the performer," Isabel said, turning to him with a wry smile.

"Excuse me?" he asked, returning the same smile.

"I saw that video of you in Asheville last year. The one on Youtube."

"Oh, man," he said, bending over and laughing. "I still don't know how that thing ended up on the Internet."

"No, you were good," she said. "I—you were good."

They looked at one another again, holding one another's stare. Finally, Spencer sat down, dangling his legs over the edge of the stage, and Isabel followed suit. She asked him about his first time performing and he admitted he was nervous like she was. "But once you lose yourself in the music, in the time that you're there, it is all good. The crowds really help because they cheer."

He asked her about her performances and she told him about singing in cafes and bars around Laurel Springs and the neighboring towns, how she never went too far from home. They didn't talk about Thomas or how they'd broken up. They didn't talk about any past relationships, but he knew it was over between them. Everyone knew.

When their conversation hit a silent moment, Isabel suddenly remembered something. She jumped up from her sitting position and got the package she'd gotten from the bookstore, the one she'd been holding onto for a week in her messenger bag, waiting to give it to Spencer.

"I'd almost forgotten about this," she said, handing him the small brown package tied with white string.

"What's this?" he asked, taking the package.

"I got this for you," she said. She sat a few feet away

from him on the stage and put her hands together between her knees. She didn't look at him, just at the present.

"For me?"

"Yeah," she said, eyes still on the package. "I know it's a week late, but I wanted to get you a present, especially since you got me one."

She actually smiled when she said it, was happy, and he didn't want to disrupt that with a negative thought. He suddenly felt worse about sleeping with Maggie now. The guilt felt like a heavy black cloak around his shoulders, made from steel or maybe lead.

"You're so sweet. You didn't have to do this," he said, still fiddling with the string.

Isabel scooted over, reached and untied it for him over his hands. She turned her face up to smile at him.

"Like I said, I wanted to," she said.

She was so close that her hair brushed against his face. He could feel how soft it was, could smell rose and lavender on her. He turned his head to the present before him, focused on tearing away the brown paper. When he pushed it away, he saw a collection of poems by Auden, entitled, *The More Loving One*. He ran his hand over the black and white image of Auden on the cover.

"This," he said, trying to find the right words to thank her. "This is great."

"I saw it in the bookstore and had to get it for you." She was smiling eagerly.

He nodded.

"Do you remember? That day on the square?"

Again, he nodded. He remembered, all right. He'd thought about that day almost every day since.

"I do."

"Do you like it?"

He looked at her, could see a bit of worry in her eyes, and suddenly realized his reaction to her gift. He loved the present, the thoughtfulness she'd put into it, to the point that it had startled him into silence that Isabel looked like she was interpreting as disappointment. No, he had to clear that up right away.

"This is perfect. I love it. Thanks, Isabel."

They both stood and he hugged her in gratitude. She hugged him back automatically. It was amazing how easy this was getting with her, which was probably why it was easy, too, when they both made a move to end the hug but didn't take their arms away from each other. They stood, just staring at one another for a long moment. She didn't pull away and neither did he.

She's Thomas's girl, Spencer thought. *Or she was, anyway.*

He leaned in a little closer to Isabel's face. She didn't move, so he leaned closer still, until their faces were only inches apart. He could feel the warmth from her face and just as he closed his eyes, could feel as she finally moved her own face forward to brush her lips against his. Their kiss was slow, lingering as their mouths moved over one another's. Spencer kept expecting Isabel to pull away, to say it wasn't right, and prayed she wouldn't. She answered him by moving her body closer, wrapping her arms around his neck, running her hands through his hair, sending sparks up the back of his neck. He responded by running his hands down her back, pleased when she shivered ever so slightly and pulled her closer, protectively, to him. They were again going somewhere where they knew nothing but one another. She was his, he was hers.

They only stopped when they heard Greg say, "Oh, oh, sorry."

Isabel jerked and looked at the stairs where Greg had just left while Spencer covered his mouth and looked toward the open field, unable to look at anyone, feeling the shock of being brought all the way back to reality at lightning-pace. He moved closer to the edge, away from everything.

Oh, man, what had he done? What was happening? She'd felt so good. And it had felt so good kissing her, like it was the most natural thing in the world to happen. It was soon, so soon after she and Thomas, and Thomas was angry. They could see that in his every act, his every word and tone.

Spencer turned back to Isabel who was standing motionless, her back to him. "I'm sorry," he said.

Isabel looked at him, her arms folded across her body now. "Yeah," she said. "Me too."

"Thank you," he said, holding up the book. He hurried past her, down the stairs. "I'll see you tomorrow."

Isabel didn't say anything more, just watched him walk away from her. They didn't say anything else to one another the rest of the night, not when they sat across from each other during the ride back to the motel, not when they unlocked their rooms, side by side of one another, but as they both lay in their beds in their darkened rooms with the sound of the ocean crashing just beyond their windows, they were the only ones who invaded one another's minds and dreams.

♬♬♬

Isabel didn't feel nervous again during rehearsals or the sound check later. She didn't feel nervous in her dressing room as she dressed, put on her makeup, warmed up her voice. No, what finally got to her was the sound of the people, hundreds and hundreds of them. They seemed to get louder with each passing second as she paced the long, dark hallway below the amphitheater where their dressing rooms were, where security safely kept them.

"Five minutes!" a man suddenly bellowed down the hallway. Isabel ran back to her and Renee's dressing room and slammed the door.

"What in the world?" Renee had been applying some bright red lipstick that accented her black, glossy hair.

"Five minutes," Isabel said. She looked at the

loveseat in their dressing room, dropped into it, then immediately got up again and started pacing. Her hands were sweaty. Her throat was dry. Oh, jeez. She went over to the dressing table and downed one of the little bottles of water that was sitting on it. Oh, jeez, now she had to reapply lipstick, she noticed as she looked in the mirror.

"Easy, easy," Renee said, taking Isabel's shaking hand that was unsuccessfully trying to reapply her lipstick. "Here, look at me."

Isabel did while Renee ran the lipstick over Isabel's lips smoothly, without a hint of shakiness.

"There, perfect," Renee said, leaning back to admire her work.

Isabel looked in the mirror. Yup, pretty damn good job. But still, all those people. She couldn't do this. She couldn't remember the songs she had to play, the words she had to sing. She got up again and started pacing. There was a bang on the door.

"Three minutes!"

Isabel turned to look at Renee. She couldn't breathe. Her stomach had been replaced with a steel trap.

"I can't do this," she said, shaking her head, putting her hands on her temples. She'd never felt this way, had never been so nervous in her life.

"Hey, hey, hey," Renee said, coming over and putting her arms around Isabel. "Settle down."

Isabel stood, letting Renee hug her. She usually didn't like to be hugged or held, and certainly didn't like drama or emotional scenes which was probably one of the reasons she was trying to escape right now, and why she didn't have many friends to hug or talk her through moments like Renee was doing right now. After a moment, she hugged Renee back. Her heart still thundered away, but she could feel her breathing slow down.

"Now," Renee said, still hugging her. "Tell me the song list for tonight, in the right order."

Isabel did.

"Good," Renee said. "Sing a couple of lines from 'Winter Rain.'"

Isabel did.

"Perfect," Renee said. "You've got this. Now, just remember, Thomas and Spence are going to do a couple of songs solo at first. All we have to do is back up at our mics on those. We take their cues. Not hard. And then you'll go into your first duet with Spencer."

They were doing two duets that night, she and Spencer.

Renee released her, but kept her hands on Isabel's arms as she said, "You'll be great. We all will."

Isabel nodded.

"Breathe," Renee commanded. Isabel obeyed.

"Don't forget to do that. Everything else will come naturally."

Isabel nodded again.

"Naturally," she repeated.

They made their way down the hall to the stairs that

led to the stage. When they joined with the guys, Renee and Greg kissed just once for luck. Spencer stared at Isabel but she couldn't look back at him. She was too busy looking at her hand clutching the cold metal railing. Her head pounded. Her chest was paralyzed.

Any minute now they'd be called on stage. She could hear the announcer talking. Thomas, who hadn't looked at her or spoken to her at all that day, except to give her instructions on stage, went first and just as he made it to the top of the stairs, she saw him switch on his smile and waved to the cheering crowd. Spencer's name was called and he leaned over to kiss Isabel's temple. Her head shot up to look at him taking the steps two at a time, but he didn't look back. He went on stage without hesitation. She touched where he'd kissed her and for the first time all day, felt herself smile. Then Greg was called on stage and Renee after. She squeezed Isabel's hand before heading up the stairs. Isabel heard her name in an unfamiliar voice and closed her eyes. When she opened them, though, something happened. She felt calm, and it was like she'd risen up and was watching herself take the stairs slowly, step on stage in front of blinding lights and wave and smile to the hundreds of cheering people who'd come there to see her and the rest of them perform. This was what she'd been waiting for since falling in love with music ten years ago. Now it was happening and on that colossal stage, as Renee smiled her way, Greg began drumming, Spencer nodded and strummed his guitar, meanwhile stomping a rhythm while even Thomas patted her shoulder and smiled as he introduced her as their newest band addition—he really should've been an actor—Isabel realized she didn't have anything to worry about. She got into the songs Spencer and Thomas did solo, never missing her backup cues on the hooks, swaying to the rhythm with Renee and when it came time for her and Spencer's duet, she took her guitar automatically and took her seat next to him at the front of the stage.

They sang the song they'd written and performed together even as they wrote it that first day in the studio. The day, every detail of it, came back to Isabel as Spencer sat across from her, his voice gliding, his eyes on hers, guiding her voice with his own. They were still locked into each other when the song ended and the audience applauded and cheered. The spell broken, they both got up and moved slightly toward one another, to the place where they'd kissed the night before. Spencer leaned a little closer, almost like he was about to repeat that kiss, but instead he just put his arm around Isabel and they both turned and waved to the crowd, the fans cheering for the best song Isabel had ever done.

Chapter 16

December 12, 2016:

Isabel could feel her body relax as he deepened the kiss. Her arms moved around him to hold him back, and she returned his kiss. All of this, what she wanted for six years from him, she returned almost automatically. She could feel it, that healing power about him. She knew what she needed to tell him. She knew he could help her. She knew he needed to know what happened six years earlier. It affected him almost as much as it did her and he didn't even know.

Awareness arose in her again and she pushed him off her, pulled herself away. Why should he know? He'd all but disappeared when she'd needed him most in their lives, leaving her to do nothing but disappear after.

"Don't do that again," she warned, still heaving, glaring into his warm blue eyes that were evident even in the dark. She didn't leave, instead stayed against the brick wall.

"Sorry," Spencer said, actually smiling. "Something I've wanted to do just about every day for six years. Forgive me for being just a little overzealous."

Isabel scoffed.

"You're crazy, you know," he said. "You almost got yourself killed walking out into the traffic like that."

Isabel looked down as she caught her breath and ran her hands through her long hair that she'd washed and blow-dried just so it would look good tonight.

Spencer's voice was quieter when he spoke again. "You really that desperate to get away from me?"

She looked at him. "You curious as to what Thomas said to me just now?"

Spencer scratched the side of his mouth with the back of his hand. "Not really," he finally answered. "But I have a pretty good idea."

"It was a warning," she continued, looking right at her former lover. Spencer put his hands in his pockets and cut his eyes over to her.

"He said that if we want this whole reunion thing to work out and be successful, then you and I need to stay away from each other."

Spencer laughed out loud this time. Isabel didn't laugh. He rubbed the back of his neck and looked at the ground for a long moment before responding.

"Still playing the wounded despot, huh?"

"So it seems," she conceded. "'Stay out of each other's pants' is the phrase he so eloquently used, I think."

Spencer turned back to her, incredulous. "He actually said that?"

Isabel nodded, turned her head to look at the lighted crepe myrtle. It was beautiful, luminous in the dark.

"I told him it wouldn't be a problem," she continued. Though even as she said that she could feel tears rising, threatening. Spencer saw them and moved closer. *Don't.* "You don't think it'll be a problem for you, do you? I mean this tryst notwithstanding. I'm sure you can stay away, can't you?"

Spencer put his hands on either side of her on the wall, encircling her, just like he was protecting her.

Isabel could feel the heat in her chest again, struggled to breathe as Spencer moved even closer, touched his forehead to hers.

"Izzy," he pleaded.

She closed her eyes. "Shouldn't be hard," she continued, feeling the tears start to roll down now. "You abandoned me to him and stayed away for six years."

"I'm sorry," he whispered.

Isabel didn't say anything, though she could. She could tell him everything he'd missed when he left, everything she'd tried to say when she tried to call him from the hospital. She'd expected to hear his voice at any time, see him walk into her room at any moment. But she never did.

And that's when the anger had settled in. Anger that led her to set out, far away so that she would never have to see either of them again. So that she would never have relive anything.

"I'm sorry," he said again.

Dear, God, what am I doing? she thought. Years of working to forget and doing a damn good job of it and now here she was, back in the presence of these two men. She shouldn't be here. She shouldn't have come back. Hadn't enough pain and anger visited for one lifetime?

"Look at me, please," he said, bringing her back to him.

Isabel opened her eyes. If she just turned her head back to him she could re-initiate their kiss and then give into everything she'd needed for the past six years. She could tell him everything, demand an explanation from him, which, she had to admit, he seemed all too willing to give. She was curious. She couldn't deny that.

He let her push his arm away, but placed a hand on her forearm before she got away completely. She turned to look at him.

"Let's get out of here," he said.

She didn't have to ask what he was saying. "I—" she began, but couldn't finish.

"Let's just go, leave, like we should've done all those years ago."

He stepped forward. She pulled away but didn't leave just yet.

"Why didn't we?" she asked.

He took another step toward her and opened his mouth to speak but she held up her hands for him to stop. She couldn't do this. Not right now. Not the moment she was thrown back into the mix with the two of them.

"Everyone's waiting," she reminded him. "To go to dinner."

He shrugged. "So?"

That one reaction, that nonchalance, did something to Isabel, made her remember everything all in one shot. She laughed, though she didn't feel the least bit funny or amused. "Well, promises mean something to *me.*"

"I came back for you, Isabel. Not for the band, not to apologize to Thomas yet again. I tried to find you. When I came back, you were gone. You never answered my phone calls. No one knew where you were. You just disappeared. Where'd you *go?*"

"Where did *you* go?" she shot back. "You disappeared too, remember? I tried to reach you and you weren't there! You left me! You left—"

She could feel the tears return and had to turn away.

"Izzy," he said, putting a hand on her face. He tried to bring her to him.

She pushed him off of her again. She couldn't do this

now. She looked away, but didn't make a move to go back into the studio. They'd been gone too long. Everyone, especially Thomas, was probably wondering what became of them. What was a few more seconds?

"Okay, then," he said, stepping back and putting his hands in his pockets. "Yeah, you're probably right. We should get back. We'll pick this up later. We're not done just yet."

He leaned in close to her face again and lowered his voice with the last word. She scowled at him and he raised his eyebrows. He began walking away, letting his arm brush against her as he did. As he got closer to the corner, he turned and walked backward a few steps so he could say, "Big day tomorrow. Hope your voice is nice and warmed up."

All Isabel could do was give him a scowl he didn't even see.

Chapter 17

November 2009:

Isabel had never been so tired and yet so wired at the same time when they got back to the hotel the night after that first show. She, the shy little girl who no one had noticed in school, had actually signed autographs and taken selfies with random strangers, answered questions about her background to a few local reporters who'd come to see the show and report it for the local paper.

It was an early show, so it was only a little after midnight as she stood on the beach now outside the hotel, letting the waves glide in over her bare feet. Salty, humid, cool air lifted her curled hair behind her and she could hear the waves roaring in the distance. She closed her eyes, feeling the wind on her skin. She almost didn't see when Spencer came into view from under the hotel lights.

She jumped but smiled, pleased to see him. He nodded as he walked toward her. He looked like he'd been working out with his hair tied back and in the long-sleeved t-shirt and sweatpants he was wearing, and wearing well, Isabel couldn't help noticing.

"Hey," she said. "Looks like I'm not the only one who wants to enjoy the beach before we leave tomorrow."

He smiled. "Yeah, know it's late, but I wanted to get in my run. Probably won't have much of a chance to in the upcoming days."

Isabel nodded, knowing what he meant. They were booked the next several days, going steadily up the coast and down to Savannah before going back up through Atlanta and a few cities in Tennessee, then back toward Columbia where Spencer said he was most looking forward to going. Not only did they have a small reprieve from touring there, but Spencer kept a cabin close to that studio where they planned to put the finishing touches on the album.

The title and the cover had been completed last week in Laurel Springs. The photographer Thomas had commissioned, an overly thin woman named Sandra with long hair and long skirts, had them walk down one of the few unpaved roads in Laurel Springs, a dirt road flanked by open fields. At one point, she had all of them stop, turn to face her. The result was them all turned or half-turned in a semi-circle, looking as if someone had interrupted a conversation. A large oak stood in the background.

"That's the one," Thomas had said as they all stood over the black and white photographs at the table at the studio two days later. He'd said as soon as he'd seen it, had barely looked at the others, and Isabel had to admit, that was yet another good decision on his part. The man knew how to run a band.

"You did really good tonight," Spencer said.

Isabel turned to smile at him, the fun and excitement of being onstage, of singing in front of everyone coming back to her.

"It was so much fun," she admitted.

They had a seat on the beach and talked a while about the show, the songs, being in front of so many people. Their conversation hit a quiet moment and Isabel, probably still high on the confidence of the show going so well, said, "So, are we going to talk about what happened yesterday?"

She wrapped her arms around her bent legs and laid her head on her knees, looking up at him sitting beside her. He laughed but didn't say anything.

The bartender from the beachfront bar made last call and just as he did, The Temptations' "My Girl" came through the speakers. They could barely hear it, but it still moved Isabel to a standing position. Everything—the show, the beach, the music, the person she was with—made her feel more alive than she had in years. She wanted to live in it as much as she could while it lasted. She held out her hands for Spencer. "Dance the shag with me."

She was already moving her feet around with the music. Spencer registered a surprised smile and took her hand, again towering over her when he stood up.

"You'll have to teach me," he said. He'd already taken her hand and put an arm around her back.

"It's easy," she said. She pulled away to demonstrate the one-two-three, four-five-six rhythm. He watched for a minute only to meet her when she did another turn and meld into the rhythm immediately with her. They danced all through the remainder of "My Girl," and then through another song and another until they lost track completely. He caught her hand, turned her at all the right moments, turned with her when the music called for it, and then, when they stopped, collapsed on the dunes in their exhaustion, breathing hard and laughing, only then did Spencer pull her face to his and kiss her. She put her hands on his forearms, strong and warm.

They took their time this time, lingering in one another as the ocean crashed from beyond. When it ended, Spencer just pulled her back to his chest and kept her in his arms as she drew her knees in, giggling when he swept her hair over her shoulder so he could kiss her neck. They said nothing more as the night wore on, no "I'm sorrys," nothing.

She fell asleep in Spencer's arms soon after, but when she woke up hours later, it was in her own bed in her own hotel room, and she almost wondered whether that time on the beach was nothing more than a dream.

Chapter 18

December 12, 2016:

It's funny, Isabel thought as she made her way back to Kat's house. All that had happened, not just to-day but over the past several years, and the one thing she couldn't stop thinking about all night was that night she and Spencer danced the shag and shared their second...or was it third?...kiss. She didn't say much at the restaurant and filled up mostly on chips and cheese dip. She had to force herself to eat that much.

Jacob asked her a couple of questions, but she could hardly hear and just nodded and forced herself to smile. Renee tried to bring her into the conversation several times but to no avail, just getting a smile and nod, also. Spencer sat at one end of the table while Thomas sat clear at the other end.

Neither spoke to her again the rest of the night, though when hers and Spencer's eyes met at one point, he did give her the briefest of smiles before turning back to his food.

Later, when Isabel unlocked the back door to Kat's, she found her sitting in the recliner watching the news, an open novel and her glasses on her lap. Her long slim legs were crossed over each other.

"How'd it go?" she asked when Isabel stepped in the room.

"Spencer kissed me," Isabel said, without missing a beat and without looking directly at Kat, instead focusing on the golden picture of Jesus on the wall above Kat's head.

"Really?" Kat sat up. "How'd that go over?"

"It was nice," Isabel admitted as she set her bag on the floor and dropped into a leather armchair opposite Kat. "Very nice. Brought back memories."

Kat laughed, gave that a moment before continuing. "Well, I would think so."

Isabel turned to her. "What do you mean?"

Kat leaned forward. "The man is only the love of your life."

Isabel groaned, closed her eyes, and sat back in her chair. Kat was always right.

"What do you think you're going to do now?"

Isabel examined her nails, began picking at one. "I don't know. I've already been doing *a lot* of thinking since that kiss. Mainly about our first show together at Myrtle Beach all those years ago."

"When you two shagged on the beach and he kissed you again?"

Isabel nodded. "That was a good moment," she said. "One of the best."

Kat set her book and glasses neatly in her lap and rubbed her hand over the novel's cover for a moment, as if pondering the artwork on it. "I'm going to tell you something," she said.

Isabel looked at her.

"I was at that first show all those years ago."

Isabel perked. "What?"

"I was," Kat nodded. "I wanted to be there to see you perform in front of all those people, and honey, you were great. Beautiful, natural, just where you were born to be."

Isabel stared at her. She couldn't believe what she was hearing. Kat had been there the whole time? "Why didn't you tell me?" Isabel asked.

"It was your moment. Not mine. I wasn't about to intrude."

Isabel half-laughed. Kat had been there, supporting her even then.

"Besides, I love any excuse to go to the beach, you know that."

Isabel laughed, feeling inexplicable tears forming.

"And I'll tell you something else, too."

Isabel looked up at her.

"Oh, I probably shouldn't say anything," Kat said, waving her hand and beginning to stand up.

"No, what?" Isabel asked, leaning forward.

"I don't want to influence your decision, but—you know I've seen a lot of concerts in my extra-long life, right?"

Isabel nodded.

"I've seen some of the great duets. Kenny Rogers and Dolly Parton, Elton John and Kiki Dee, Marvin Gaye and Tammi Terrell and—I know I'm biased, but you two sounded just exquisite together. Beautiful."

Isabel felt herself blush, even now.

"Your voices were *made* to sing together, hon. And the way you two looked at each other. Well, it was obvious you were in love, even then."

Isabel brought her hand to her mouth. "Are you serious?"

All the looks she and Spencer had exchanged before. It was no wonder Thomas still held such hostility. Everything was so obvious.

Kat nodded in answer to her question. "It was the same look you have right now."

Isabel sighed and Kat put her hand over Isabel's.

"And if you want to take the advice of an old woman who hasn't been the luckiest in love—"

She paused dramatically and Isabel laughed.

"Talk to him. Tell him what happened all those years ago. Let him tell you, too. And that spark that's still between you? Let it come to life."

That was the last thing she said before bidding Isabel good night and turning in, but Isabel stared after her a long time afterward, wondering just how right her cousin was.

Chapter 19

January 2010:

Isabel followed Spencer outside, saw him swing his leg over the side of his motorcycle just as she was pushing open the heavy glass door. She called to him just before he started it up and he turned his head, sat back as he waited for her to approach. She slowed to an almost hesitant walk down the cobblestone walkway. Neither said anything for a long time.

"Wh—where are you going?" she finally asked, folding her arms across her chest. He looked at the road ahead, at the mountains in the distance.

"Thought I'd just go for a ride." He didn't look at her

as he said it, and Isabel surmised he wanted to be alone, just as she would after what had gone down.

Twenty minutes earlier everything was fine. Thomas had rented out that small studio outside of Columbia to put some finishing touches on the songs before releasing the album officially.

Everything was going fine.

They were doing the final run through when, bam: "We're going make this one a solo," Thomas said.

Spencer and Isabel looked at him. He didn't look at either of them, only at the paper before him, the millions of little controls and buttons and switches in that studio. He was talking about their song, the first one they did together.

Spencer turned a fraction of an inch in Thomas's direction.

Thomas still didn't look at him, at anyone. "Isabel can do it alone. It works good alone. Better."

"The song is two people conversing," Spencer said. His voice was calm, steady, but the blue fire in his eyes burned a little brighter. "It won't work as a solo."

"It will," Thomas said with finality.

"I don't know," Renee said, moving to look at the lyrics. "It's great as a duet, and the crowd loves it. Why would we change it?"

"Because I said so," Thomas snapped, staring at Renee.

She moved back to her place next to Greg.

"Hey, you don't need to talk to her that way," Greg said.

"This is my band," Thomas said. "Every decision, every song, everyone who plays or sings or does anything for this band is under me! Do you understand? These are not your decisions! I know what is best, and you don't take what is mine! Not you, not her, no one! Do you understand?" His anger was real and directed at Greg, as evidenced by him moving toward his drummer, but Greg was only the punching bag, Isabel could see. Everything Thomas was wanting to say to Spencer, he was saying to Greg.

"Thomas!" Spencer stepped in, put a hand on the chest of his red-faced friend.

Thomas looked at him and knocked his hand away. "You say nothing!"

"Yeah, I think that's been the problem for far too long," Spencer said. "This is your band, yeah, but you don't dictate what we do and don't do, especially if it affects the goodness of a song, one that could be a potential hit, could do us well. And you sure as hell don't get up in the face of someone whose been nothing but loyal to you since he started. Come on, man, what the hell is wrong with you?"

Thomas said nothing for a long second, one in which Isabel thought that maybe, just maybe, she saw a calmness come over, in which she thought everything would be just fine. Thomas turned toward the controls for a sec-

208 Tanya Newman

ond, but only so he could get enough power and enough surprise to slam his fist right across Spencer's jaw in the next second.

Spencer doubled back a half-step. "Son of a bitch!" he yelled. He grabbed Thomas's shirt and threw him up against the wall.

"Spencer!" Renee, Greg, and Isabel all shouted at once, their hands on him and Thomas, trying to push them apart.

Spencer looked at Thomas a long moment before shoving him against the wall a last time, whipping around, taking one of the guitars, and smashing it into the wall.

They all looked at the wreckage in his wake as the door slammed behind him. It was the loudest silence Isabel had ever heard. She looked at Thomas who had his eyes narrowed right at her. For two months they'd toured up and down the South Carolina and Georgia coasts then back up through Atlanta and Tennessee before coming back into central and upstate Carolina.

Spencer and Isabel kept their moments together brief, elusive—a kiss before going onstage after everyone else had gone, walking along the battery in Charleston in the middle of the night. Things never really progressed beyond that, but Isabel didn't mind for some reason. Just like their first meeting on that balcony that night in September, it was just as exciting hovering on the edge of the fire. They were careful. But still, Thomas must have seen something. The way he was looking at her, he must have seen something.

She glared at him before following Spencer outside where she now stood before him as he sat on his motorcycle.

"Where are you going?" she asked.

"As it so happens, I know someone in the next town. A good friend. Thought I'd ride around, blow off steam, crash there tonight."

Isabel nodded. That sounded like just the right idea.

"Be careful," she only offered, taking a step back, preparing to go back inside, though she knew she wouldn't. She didn't know where she was going to go.

"You want to join me?" she heard him ask and turned just as a slight breeze lifted her hair off of her shoulders. He was looking at her now.

She swallowed once. She'd never found it easy to speak or even read her own thoughts. Everything always seemed too jumbled and complex to find. But right now it was easy.

"Yes."

He moved forward on the bike so she could get on behind him. She put her arms around him, nestled herself against his strong back, as if she'd done it a thousand times before, as if she were born to do it.

She'd never been on a motorcycle before. The rush of the wind blowing her hair behind her, flying past the pine trees, unguarded by the windows or doors of a car, pure freedom, yet holding onto him because he was the lifeline that kept her from falling, she began to understand why people chose to ride these things, how easy it would be to slip and fall, to fall in love. That's when she knew.

If she hadn't been in love with Spencer before then, she was now. She looked up, closing her eyes to the sun, forgetting her bearings, holding on tight to him. She had no idea where they were and didn't care. It was a resplendent day, cool and sunny at the same time, the sky a warm sapphire and they were rapidly passing fields of fenced-in green, some of the most beautiful country she'd ever seen. Occasionally they'd pass a farmhouse or a field of statuesque horses grazing contentedly.

Finally, he slowed and turned onto a blacktop driveway that was flanked by a seemingly endless forest. The trees masked the sky so that it became almost immediately darkened and cooler. Isabel couldn't help but straighten up and stiffen just a little as the darkness surrounded them and they pressed forward, away from civilization, away from anything—

Where were they going?

Isabel wanted to ask again, but stayed quiet, taking in the forest around them. Finally, they rounded a curve and the driveway opened to a seemingly endless field. There was a red barn standing close to a white, two-story farmhouse. The field behind the barn was fenced in and Isabel could see a few horses grazing or walking about. A small, red foal with spindly legs stood close to its mother near one end.

She heard Spencer laugh in her direction and suddenly took notice of how she was leaning forward over him, eagerly looking at the scenery.

"You like this place?" he asked.

She smiled at him, nodding in response. Spencer stopped the motorcycle in the driveway that curved in front of the old house, and that's when Isabel noticed a tall, weather-beaten man with white hair, probably in his mid-fifties, leaning against a smaller paddock, watching a sleek black horse prance back and forth for his audience, as if he knew what a sight he was.

Spencer killed the engine, put the kickstand down and got off the cycle.

"Uncle Jack!" he called, waving to the man, who turned around and called Spencer by name.

The two men hugged and Jack clapped Spencer on the back a couple of times. They laughed and said something Isabel couldn't quite hear just yet. She slowly got off the motorcycle and began walking toward the two men, aware of where they were now.

"This is Isabel," Spencer said, turning and putting a hand on her back.

"Isabel," Jack said in greeting, nodding to her with a friendly smile.

"Nice to meet you," she said, smiling in return. "This place is amazing."

"It keeps the rain off my head," Jack said.

Isabel smiled again and turned to Spencer. "You grew up here?"

"Since I was ten," he said. "Jack, here, taught me everything I know about horses as well as music."

"Ah, I'm not taking too much credit," Jack said, waving Spencer away. "That boy taught himself to play most of the instruments he knows."

"Wouldn't have if you hadn't introduced me."

Jack turned to Isabel. "So, you just joined the band? How're you liking it? This fellow here and everyone treating you all right?"

Isabel laughed and told him yeah to everything. They talked for a while about the band and touring until the black horse stopped prancing and pawed the ground, aware that he wasn't the center of attention anymore. Isabel nearly jumped back, seeing the horse standing so close to her. Wow, that thing was immense when she was standing this close to it.

She looked at Spencer and pointed at the black steed. "I hope you're not expecting me to get on that thing."

He laughed. "Only if you want."

He easily walked over to the horse and patted him on the neck, who returned the sentiment by nuzzling Spencer's chest and tossing his own head a few times.

"Think he missed me," he said to Jack, and Jack laughed.

"Yeah, it's been a while," Jack said.

"Wait a minute," Isabel said, puzzled. "That horse is yours?"

"Yeah," Spencer said, scratching the horse between the ears and taking the lead rope from Jack. "His name is Eclipse. Raised him from a foal. First one I ever trained on my own. Jack said it was only fair I got to keep him. Haven't seen him in…what's it been, Jack? A year?"

"Nearly," Jack said. "You think you can remember how to do this?"

"Think so," Spencer answered, patting the horse on the neck a couple of more times.

Wow, Isabel thought. She knew Spencer had grown up here, knew how to ride horses. But, it was completely different seeing him in action. He was so easy with the horse, like he'd taken care of them all his life.

Oh, wait, Isabel thought. *He has.*

Spencer turned toward Isabel, motioned for her to come closer. Isabel tried, but couldn't seem to work the muscles required for her to move forward.

"He won't hurt you," Spencer promised, rubbing the horse's neck. "You can pet him if you want."

His words were inviting, not forceful. Isabel looked at the animal before her, meeting its eyes that were so brown they were almost as black as his coat. He blinked softly a few times, looking right through her, and very slowly, she reached up and stroked his nose, finding it to be as soft as velvet. The horse puffed a few times onto her hand, his breath warm. Isabel half-giggled at him.

"That's it," Spencer encouraged. "Gently."

Isabel stroked his nose again and he puffed more on-to her hand.

"He's getting a sense of you," Spencer said. "Saying hello."

"Hmm," Isabel said, crossing her arms again, still smiling at the horse before her.

He never shied away, never showed any signs of fear or hostility, only a calm which Isabel felt transferring to her.

"He's beautiful," she said.

"You want to help me groom him?" Spencer asked.

"Um," Isabel said, unsure of what he meant, exactly. She didn't know if she was ready to ride just yet, but he hadn't said that, so—

"Just brush him down, comb his mane and tail," he clarified and she could hear Jack laugh at her naiveté, and she found herself laughing, too. Spencer turned back to her for an answer and she shrugged and so he said, "Come on."

He led her and Eclipse alongside him to the barn and they went inside. A few other horses eyed them from their stalls as they walked through the cavernous building that was lit only by a few dim bulbs overhead and the sun peeking in from the doorways and windows. Finally, Spencer stopped about halfway through the building and clipped two ropes, attached on either side of the wall, to each side of Eclipse's halter. He started rummaging through a red bucket that was off to the side and pulled out a round rubber brush. He tossed it upward once and called it a curry comb.

Isabel raised her eyebrows once to let him know she hadn't the faintest idea what that was.

"I'll show you how it works," he said.

He placed the brush in her hand and then, standing behind her, placed his hand over hers and began massaging it into the horse's neck. Isabel tried to focus on the task at hand, but found herself distracted by the warmth of Spencer's hand and over hers, his arm over her arm.

"This loosened the dirt from his coat," Spencer said into her ear, and Isabel could feel the chills move down her neck, causing an almost involuntary smile. Spencer kissed the side of her face, then, making her turn in his direction. Spencer looked at her with those dark eyes of his like he was searching for something, and after a minute gave up and leaned in to kiss her, just once, before saying, "Come on, let's finish up."

They finished grooming Eclipse and by the time they did, the horse's coat was gleaming. Spencer saddled Eclipse and put a tangle of leather straps over the horse's head. He called that a bridle.

"Sure you don't want to ride?"

"I'm sure," Isabel said.

Spencer laughed as he took the reins and led the horse outside, taking Isabel's hand. When they reached the outside again, Spencer let go and put the reins over

Eclipse's head. Then he jumped straight up, caught the stirrup with his foot and flung his other leg over.

"Whoa," she said, standing back a second too late. "How'd you do that?"

He gave her a confused look for a second and then, realizing what she meant, just shrugged and laughed. "Just picked it up when I was learning to ride."

"It's no wonder," she said, folding her arms across her chest.

"How's that?' he asked.

"You're good at everything you do," she clarified.

Spencer just rolled his eyes in response.

"Come on," she said. "Stop playing coy. You can't tell me you don't know."

It took him a moment to respond. He adjusted the reins in his hands and said, "Well, I guess like a lot of people I do my best. I'm just damn well not going to boast about a thing. Now—" He leaned down and held out his hand for her to take. "Come on," he said. "I'll keep you safe. You're my girl."

Isabel could feel herself go still when he said that, though the expression could be trite or even possessive. It just didn't feel that way coming from him. It felt nice, him thinking of her that way, and she knew she'd always thought of him as hers, too. That was why no other romantic relationship had ever worked out in her life. Deep down, she'd always known that and now, seeing him looking at her with his hand outstretched for her to take, that knowledge rose to the surface along with the reality that this wasn't just a crush anymore. Maybe it never was.

Isabel took his hand. He took his foot out of the stirrup so she could place hers in it, and with his help, she hoisted herself onto the horse.

He may not feel the same way, a voice warned her. *This may be just a casual thing for him.*

But even as Isabel heard and understood the words in her mind, she placed her arms around Spencer midsection, holding on tight as he nudged the horse into a walk and, feeling the warmth and strength of his back against her, she didn't feel one ounce of panic or worry.

♫♫♫

Isabel and Spencer spent the rest of the day at his uncle's ranch. Spencer walked her around, pointed out how far the land went, the lake and the cabin that was his on the other side. He knew all the horses by breed and name. When they got back, they found Jack had grilled steaks and had potatoes out and had everything set and ready to eat on the kitchen table. Isabel tried to help clean up after, but he got out his old guitar, told her to have a seat and play him a song. She did without a hint of nervousness and she and Spencer sang the song they'd written together, the one they'd played about a hundred times onstage together by now. When Jack stretched and got up, he hugged Isabel and told her he enjoyed meeting her.

"Thank you," she said, returning his hug as if he were her own uncle. "This has been one of the best days I can remember."

Jack told them he was going to turn in but that they were welcome to hang out as long as they wanted. Spencer stood but told Isabel to keep her seat, he'd be right back. She could see him talking low to Jack as they made their way upstairs and Jack nodded, saying something back, but she couldn't make out what they were saying, exactly. Shrugging, she took in the old kitchen. The floors were hardwood and the appliances looked like they were from the 1940s, with a handle on the refrigerator that you actually had to pull down own to get it to open. She made her way to the living room, noticing the immense television looking like it was from only a couple of decades later.

She smiled. She liked the antique yet sturdy feeling the house exuded. She felt like she could spend the rest of her life right here with Spencer. She made her way to the front dining room, darkened and housing a lone baby grand piano. Isabel walked over, played a few notes with one hand.

"That was nice," she heard Spencer say from behind and she turned around to find him leaning against the doorframe. He stared at her and she at him, and she became astoundingly aware that they were alone, with no one around to interrupt them. They could do anything they wanted.

Spencer looked at a small box in his hand before pocketing it and coming over to where Isabel was standing. He held out his hand, and she took it. He twirled her around, brought her back to him and kissed her.

"Been wanting to do that since the night we met," he said.

"I wanted you to," she admitted.

He touched his forehead to hers. "Hey, you want to see something pretty great?"

"Sure, I'm in the mood," she said.

He took her hand and led her back outside to where his motorcycle was still parked. They got on and drove along the smooth dirt road that ran alongside the lake, from the large farmhouse to the small cabin at the other end. It was dark, but Jack had installed a few outside lights to illuminate the way. Enormous pines stretched all around beyond the lake and behind the cabin.

"There," Spencer pointed at the lake.

The ripples caught the light from the moon just right, make it look like small sparkles in the darkness. It was lovely.

"Hmm," Isabel said, laying her head on his back. "It's beautiful."

The air was cold all around, light. He sat for a long time there, in front of her. He didn't turn around, didn't say anything, so she made a move to remove her arms from around him, but he caught her hand, kept it where it was.

She sighed and closed her eyes when he did that, felt a smile come forth. The lovely electricity moved through her and she turned her head to the side and rested it on his shoulder.

Spencer turned his head, spoke in a low voice though he didn't have to, though they were the only ones there.

"He got to you before I did. Thomas."

Isabel didn't open her eyes. "No, he didn't."

Spencer sat up, then, and turned around to face her. He took his time as he reached up, ran his hand down the side of her face, much like he had the night they'd met. Isabel closed her eyes, smiled, enjoyed his touch. He kept his hand on her face as he leaned in to kiss her, drew her closer so he could put his arms fully around her. She found herself gripping his back with both hands as if he might vanish if she didn't. And when he ended the kiss, as slowly as he'd started, he kept her close, and she didn't open her eyes, didn't let him go, just turned her face into his neck.

She didn't want to ruin the moment, but had to know something. "Why?"

"It was time," he said into her ear. "Besides..." He pulled away, turned his face so he could look into her eyes. "...before recently, you were taken."

She closed her eyes, shrank a little.

"Don't think I blame you for that."

She shook her head. "I know you don't. I'm still sorry because I don't know what else to be."

He shrugged. "Just wasn't the right time."

"Maybe not," she agreed.

He sighed, looked over at the lake in the distance for a minute before turning back to her and saying, "Stay with me?"

She knew what he was asking, and she nodded.

Spencer's cabin was all wood, well-kept with a chimney made from stone. The sky was dark and the air was cool, crisp, and as they got off his motorcycle and went inside. It was dark inside, so she couldn't see much but not that she would've had a chance to, anyway. As soon as he closed the door behind them, he took her hand and pulled her to him all in one motion so he could kiss her again.

That's when she knew no more words were needed between them. Still having hold of her hand, he led her inside, to his room and his bed. She always found herself nervous in that moment before, but now, just like when he'd kissed her, she didn't. Just as their voices had been made to sing together, she found that their bodies and souls had been made to be together. And in the hours after, before drifting into sleep, she lay against him under the protective embrace of his arm, and had never felt more complete, at peace, and alive, ever.

♫ ♫ ♫

When Isabel awoke the next morning, it was to the sun streaming in delicately from the blinds and the sound of a hawk in the distance. Spencer wasn't there, but she could smell coffee. She sat up and stretched, feeling the chill of winter that had settled in all around, and pulled the deep blue fluffy covers around her. She closed her eyes to it all, felt herself smiling genuinely for the first time in a long time.

I want to stay here, just like this. Forever.

She wondered how long it would take Spencer to come back to bed if she just stayed where she was, and felt her smile widen even more at the thought of him doing that. She considered it until a rumbling of hunger in her stomach disagreed. She groaned, getting up and dressing back in her jeans and long-sleeved white t-shirt, taking a look around. The bed was oak, with ornate carvings on the headboard that she hadn't seen in the darkness last night. The walls were the same oak wood of the outside cabin, offset by stone accents. The ceilings were high in the living room and the fireplace was immense and made entirely from stone. Floor-to-ceiling windows and French doors showed a view of the rolling hills and pines in the distance that they'd not been able to see from the road.

She found a ceramic mug in one of the glass cabinets in the kitchen and poured herself some coffee, noting how good and strong it was. There was a natural taste to it too, unlike store-bought kinds. She was making her way to the front door that stood slightly ajar when she stopped short, hearing Spencer's voice. And Thomas's.

"Where is she?" Thomas asked. He sounded like he was on the edge of a cliff. She knew that tone. She closed her eyes, feeling her heart beat in her chest.

"Morning," Spencer replied.

"Damn it, Spence, I know she's here. I was watching from the window. I saw her leave with you."

"So, you're a spy now?" Spencer mused.

"*What happened?*"

Isabel was still as fast, hard footsteps she knew were Spencer's approached. His voice was low, threatening as he spoke. "Something that started before you even made a move on her."

"What the hell are you talking about?"

Spencer didn't answer. She could hear footsteps again and knew he'd turned away, that he didn't want this fight that Thomas was seemingly determined to have.

"Started before I made a move on her? So I guess this is like some prior claim, then?"

Still no answer.

"Tell me, does she know about you? Your past? About all the others? All the other women who'd just *love* to be in her position, now? Who *have* been in her position? What's she going to think about that?"

She could hear as Spencer whipped around. "Don't you dare start in on me or judge me, Thomas, when you cheated on her with your ex and lied to her practically the whole time you were with her. What do you care, any-way, if you and Jessie are back together now?"

"I never said we were back together. I made a mis-take."

"For two months straight?"

"You know you don't deserve her."

Isabel rolled her eyes. Of course, changing around the subject to reflect the other's mishaps. Thomas was good at that.

Spencer paused a moment, probably taking another sip of coffee, before continuing. "I may be the so-called playboy of the group and I may have spent my share of time with women, but they were *all* just *one at a time*. I never cheated and I never lied about who I am. Isabel knows that."

"Well, good for you," Thomas drilled on. "Aren't you the better man, the saint? So I guess you're just a re-formed little man who's going to marry her now?"

Isabel felt her breath catch a little. They hadn't—no one had even mentioned that word. *How dare Thomas say that?*

"If she'll have me."

Isabel had to catch her coffee mug with the other hand to keep it from toppling to the ground and shatter-ing. *Oh, my...*

"If she'll—" Thomas began to repeat Spencer's words before choking on his own bitter laughter.

Isabel swallowed hard, feeling the sting of tears. He

really was enjoying this, getting to Spencer. She could tell. But it was the next statement that hurt the worst.

"You can't take care of her, and you know it."

Spencer didn't hesitate. "I love her."

Thomas laughed again before saying, "Well, you know what? You two can just try this, whatever it is, on your own, then."

She heard Thomas step off the porch, begin walking to his car. Spencer stayed on the porch. He leaned over the railing, took another sip of coffee before saying, "What's that supposed to mean?"

"What do you think it means?" Thomas was yelling again, and Isabel moved closer to the door.

"You two keep this up, you're gone. Out of *my* band, the one *I* started."

Isabel stepped out onto the porch now, ready to face them both and end this. But, as both men turned to look at her, she froze all over again.

She let her eyes fall on the only man she'd ever loved before turning to Thomas.

"Thomas," she began, hoping she could talk to him, calm him somehow.

"No, you don't talk!" he said, point a finger at her. He started walking toward her, but Spencer moved protectively in front of her.

"Leave her out of this," he said to Thomas.

"Leave her out of this?" Thomas repeated, his hollow laugh erupting once again. "She's the whole reason 'this' started! I found her! I recruited her! You have no right to steal her away. She's mine!"

Isabel raised her eyebrows.

No one said a word for a long time. Then Thomas threw his hands up in exasperation, began walking toward his car. Before getting in, he turned to them to say one more thing: "So, the two little lovers, it seems, have some thinking to do. You want to stay with the band or together. It's up to you. Spencer, I thought you were my friend. I did, man."

Spencer said nothing.

"And you," Thomas said, shifting his eyes to Isabel. It was like he couldn't even utter her name. "Well, you just enjoy the ride. I know a lot of other women have."

Isabel turned her eyes to the ground.

"Thomas, get in your car and get out of here," Spencer said, and Thomas did, but not before waving to both of them, the damage done.

They both stood, watching in the distance long after Thomas's car disappeared from view. Finally, Isabel took a step toward Spencer's back, put one hand on his shoulder, the other on his strong forearm. He turned his head to the side, toward, her, in response. She looked up at him.

"Hi," she said, and he half-laughed.

He turned around, took her in his arms and kissed her. "Not exactly the way I wanted this morning to go."

"Hmm," she said into his chest. "It was inevitable, I guess. What's going to happen now?"

"Well, I'd like to say Thomas will come around, but you know him."

Isabel closed her eyes against Spencer's chest. She knew they needed to think and talk about what Thomas had said, but she just didn't want to right then.

"Not as well as you know him," she admitted. "Do you think I should go talk to him?"

"He's in a dark place," Spencer said. "He needs time." He took a minute before continuing, looked out at the lake now illuminated with the light of the sun shining down, so unlike the darkness from the night before. "I should've known better than to bring you here. Should've known he'd come looking here."

Isabel pushed herself to him even more, inhaled his earthy scent. "So, what are we going to do?"

He leaned down so he could whisper in her ear. "I think we may have to postpone this a while—"

Isabel jerked away, looked at him fiercely. "I've waited since we met—I can't—I don't—"

She shook her head, backing away.

"I just mean in front of everyone, just for a while until it seems he's calmed down about this some."

Isabel had turned away from him. But now she didn't see the beauty of the pines in the distance. She grimaced as the puzzle pieces of what he was saying started coming together in her mind.

"You mean—" she began, turning her head just to the side.

He nodded. "Just lay low for a while." He began moving toward her, and she let him approach, let him run his hands down her back and encircle her waist. He nuzzled her neck. "Because in case you haven't noticed, I've been waiting, too. And I'll be damned if I'm going to give you up now, even for a little while."

He turned her around so he could kiss her again.

"This is not going to be easy," she continued. *Pretending I'm not with you, that I don't love you. It was hard enough pretending I didn't love you before.*

"No," he conceded as he touched his forehead to hers. "But at least we don't have to stay apart all the time. The band will be expected to be together most of the time on this upcoming tour. And don't forget—"

She smiled now, put her arms around him. "We'll all be staying in the same places."

"There will be lots of moments like this. I'll see to it."

"Hmm, you'd better."

He laughed at that then reached into his jeans pocket and pulled out a small black box. He held it up to Isabel. It was tiny, black velvet.

"What is this?" she asked, feeling a pang of panic in her stomach. *If she'll have me…*

"This is something that belonged to my aunt," Spencer clarified. "She and my uncle never had kids, not a daughter to pass it to, not a son to give to his girl. Jack gave it to me one day and told me that. He said if I ever met a girl I wanted to give it to, I could. I always kept it here, because, well, there was never a girl I felt strongly enough about to give a family heirloom like this."

Isabel couldn't move. She stared at Spencer. She didn't know about this.

"It's not an engagement ring." He laughed. "But it's something that means a lot to my family."

Isabel curled her lips under and finally opened the box. Inside was a ring of three slim bands, silver or white gold, she couldn't tell. They were connected with tiny sprinkled light blue stones all around. Isabel took it from the box. It fit her right ring finger perfectly.

"It's beautiful," Isabel said, admiring it. "Aquamarines?"

"Blue diamonds," Spencer answered, taking her hand to look at the ring on it.

"Spencer!" Isabel said, realizing the value and magnitude of the ring. "This is too much, I can't—"

Spencer stopped her, shaking his head and taking her right hand in both of his own so he could bring it to his mouth. "My granddaddy gave it to my grandma, the woman he loved more than anything, all his life. When she died, he gave it to uncle who gave it to my Aunt Mellie, and then when she passed away, he gave it to me."

Isabel swallowed hard.

"It has always ended up on the hand of a woman that a man in my family loved," Spencer continued.

Isabel couldn't speak, but she didn't have to.

Spencer finished with, "That's why you should have it."

She sighed, looking again at how the stones glittered in the morning light and knew this was a ring she wasn't going to take off.

"Thank you," she said.

Chapter 20

December 13, 2016:

Isabel?"

She heard him call to her but didn't turn around right away. It was a little after six, but she'd been awake for hours already, finally giving up on sleep, leaving Kat a note and taking a walk in the dawn light that ended her right on the Dagnall Bridge. She didn't know how long she'd been standing there with her hands deep in the pockets of her long dark jacket, watching the Little River ebb and flow below.

When she did turn around, she saw Spencer standing several feet away. He'd been running, obviously, just like she had the feeling he might be at that hour, judging from what she'd seen a couple of days earlier.

"Hi," he said.

"Hi."

"You're out early."

"So are you."

He smirked. Then, he pointed toward the little two lane road that led back to the square.

"You want some coffee? I know a good place. We could walk back there while we wait for the awkwardness to pass over."

Isabel stood where she was a moment.

"Unless..." He began backing away a few steps, still looking at her.

"No, coffee sounds great," she said, falling into step beside him.

They didn't say much as they walked back to the square. It was still quiet, as most businesses weren't open, yet. Isabel was surprised when he took a key from his pocket and unlocked the door to the coffee shop. He flipped a switch on the wall, letting the lights illuminate the echoing room. There was a long coffee bar that stretched the length of the shop, set across from several two-seater tables. Various abstract paintings hung on the walls. A little framed chalkboard sign on the counter read, *Singer/guitarist wanted. Four nights a week.*

"Sorry, it's a little chilly," he said, hitting a switch in the back. Isabel could hear the heat come to life as he came back to the front and started the coffee at one of the several coffee pots that lined behind the bar.

"You work here?" she asked.

Spencer laughed. "You might say that. I own the place."

She could feel her jaw drop. "What? For how long?"

Spencer folded his arms, looked at the ceiling as he thought. "About three years now."

Three years? Isabel thought about that. She'd been home every Christmas to see Kat. She'd never missed a year. And somewhere in those last three years, Spencer had been in Laurel Springs, her place, her hometown.

"Why?" she asked. "Why here? Why didn't you keep making music?"

"Didn't say I stopped making music," he said. The coffee pot finished brewing behind him and he reached below and pulled out two beige mugs.

"Scott will be here in about a half-hour," he said as the coffee finished up. Isabel had been looking at a painting of solid blue when he said that. She had a seat at the bar. He put a little stainless steel container of creamer in front of her, knowing that was all she took in her coffee. He stood on the other side of the bar as they both sipped, looking at the day get a little brighter outside, the occasional car pass by.

"I'm sorry I was a little forward last night," he said, making her look his way. He had a half-smile that she couldn't help returning. He could still make her do that.

"I just missed you," he continued. He took a sip of his coffee, looked outside and then at the glossy counter. "I still love you, you know."

Isabel felt a catch in her chest. She looked back at him, stared at him for a long time before getting up off the stool and going to stand in front of the window. What was she supposed to say to that? That she loved him, too? And then what would happen? They'd forget everything and live happily ever after?

She turned around at long last. "Is that why you didn't return my calls? Why you just disappeared?"

Spencer ran a hand through his hair before coming around the bar and placing his hands in his pockets.

"I—" he began but Isabel held up her hands.

"I didn't come here to get into it. I—" *Just tell him. Get on with it. Tell him and leave. It's why you came here, isn't it?* Isabel turned, looked all around, and folded her arms. "This place is beautiful. You've done a great job."

He didn't break eye contact. "Thank you."

She looked at him a long time.

"What *did* you come here to say?" he asked, finally.

Isabel curled her lips under and looked at the floor for a moment before she finally met his eyes again and let the moment flicker to life.

Chapter 21

March 2010:

Two days later, Isabel took a slow sip of her coffee as she stood in front her bathroom mirror in her apartment. They were back in Laurel Springs, set to begin work on another album. She squinted as she examined her face, seeing the flaws like she always did but hardly able to pick up her powder, her blush, her mascara to fix them. She pushed her palms onto the counter, looked at the sink before her. Nerves again. Reasons different this time.

She was where she belonged—alone—if she wanted to keep her job.

"But not forever," she reminded herself in the mirror.

Her hands were shaking as she waved the mascara wand over her lashes and she ended up stabbing herself in the eye, like she knew she would. She cursed, as the stinging encapsulated her eyeball, and splashed some water in it. She had to go sit on her bed and put her face in her hands a few minutes.

And now she'd have to re-do her face that had already taken the better part of fifteen minutes. She sighed, hearing a knock at the door, knowing that was probably Renee. She looked down as she answered, hiding her mess of a face.

"Thought we could walk over together," Renee said. Greg stood behind her, waved in greeting.

"Hi," she returned. "I'm not quite ready." She half-spoke, half-whispered, trying to smile. "Sorry. Just a few more minutes. Do you mind getting me a latte?"

"No problem," she said.

She nodded, thanked them before closing the door. She was still looking down and noticed that she'd put on one black boot and one red. Sighing, she took off the black one, threw it across the room, and shoved her foot into the other red one. She finished her face in a hurry, in a heap of angry adrenaline, grabbed her bag, and took one last look around.

She was ready, but still waited a few more minutes, watching the Laurel Springs traffic below. She'd be damned if she were early and had to sit in a room alone with Thomas, waiting on the others to get there. She felt her shoulders drop as she saw her clothes and the black boot she'd thrown still lying on the floor. She picked the items up and dropped them in her closet. She just hated to leave a mess behind.

♫♫♫

"She's not usually this late."

Greg looked at Renee.

"Isabel," Renee clarified. They were waiting on the barista at the coffee shop finish up Isabel's latte and their coffees, too.

Greg laughed. "I know who you're talking about."

The barista handed them their coffees and Renee paid. She turned back to Greg as he got the tray of drinks.

"She seemed different, like she wasn't really…okay, this morning."

Greg just looked at her sideways.

"I mean, she was still sweet and everything, but…I don't know."

He nudged her shoulder. "You worry too much, my love. Whatever's wrong, Spencer will take care of her."

Renee shrugged. It was true. Everyone pretty well knew that Isabel and Spencer were together now. But shouldn't that be a happy thing?

♫♫♫

Thomas, Greg, and Renee were sitting on the floor in the cavernous studio when Isabel walked in. They all looked at her, and she paused, still holding the door handle, fully aware she could turn around, could walk out and away, wait for Spencer downstairs and tell him she'd changed her mind. She couldn't do this anymore, carry on a charade. It had gotten to the point in the last couple of weeks that he wouldn't even call her or come to her room in the evening time. They should just leave, make a clean break, a change. It was morning, her favorite time of day, when the day and the world were still full of possibilities of change.

Isabel swallowed once, closed the door behind her. Her hand was stiff from having held the door handle so tightly for so long. Without a word she handed Thomas the lyrics to the four songs she'd finished up and thought were in good enough shape. Without a word and barely a glance, he took them, looked them over as she set her large black handbag down and uncinched her coat from around her waist. She thanked Renee for the latte and had a seat as far away as she could get and still be in the group. Greg examined the lyrics with Thomas. Renee stared at Isabel and when Isabel didn't respond, Renee, ever the caretaker, placed her hand on Isabel's arm. Tears came forth almost immediately, and she shook her head at Renee.

"We're talking later," Renee informed her in a whisper.

Isabel nodded just as the door swung open and in stepped Spencer, shielded by his own sunglasses. His messenger bag was crossed over his tall, lion-esque frame. Even his dark hair, thick and long, was like a lion's mane, Isabel couldn't help noticing for about the hundredth time.

Despite being nearly a half-hour late, he took his time closing the door behind him and coming into room. He slung his bag onto the floor, handed Thomas his own work, and sat down right next to him.

"You're late," Thomas said in response.

"You're perceptive." Spencer stretched his arms forward and rested his head on his elbows. No one saw when he and Isabel removed their sunglasses at the same time—their sign, their way of telling one another in plain sight that they loved each other. Spencer winked at her a millisecond before Thomas turned to him, started telling him exactly what was wrong with his compositions on the songs. Not that anything was. Thomas was pointing out nitpicky BS, Isabel could see, and she could see from Greg and Renee's exchange of glances that they thought the exact same thing. She tried to watch without looking as Spencer still sat back on his elbows, listening to everything Thomas said without protest.

Her mind drifted…

'*I think we may have to postpone this a while…*'

'*I've waited since we met… I can't…I don't…*'

'*I just mean in front of everyone, just for a while un-*

*til it seems he's…calmed down about this some. Just lay
low for a while. Because in case you haven't noticed, I've
been waiting, too. And I'll be damned if I'm going to give
you up now, even for a little while.'*

"…and I'm making a small change to this one,"
Thomas said, holding up the composition on the latest of
songs she and Spencer were to sing a duet on. "I think it
should be a solo."

Spencer sat up, looked at the song. "It won't make
sense," he said. "It's a conversation, going back and
forth."

Thomas held up his hand for Spencer to stop as he
scribbled furiously. Spencer looked up at the ceiling,
rolled his eyes. No fights this time. Minutes later, Thomas thrust the new lyrics in Isabel's direction. "Think you
can handle that, sweetie?" He popped his pen closed.

Isabel felt a small twitch on the side of her face. She
picked up the lyrics, looked them over. Yes, Thomas had
indeed all but cut out Spencer's part, had made it all hers,
changed a lot of "you's" in the lyrics to "I" and so forth,
so it would make sense being a solo rather than a duet.
But it killed a little something. There was no fiery pas-
sion in it anymore, only anger now. It wouldn't work
nearly as well, wouldn't be the hit they'd imagined.

"Well," Isabel began, still looking at the paper.
"Yeah, but—"

"Good enough," he cut in. "I'll back you up on the
chorus, got it?"

Her shoulders and the paper dropped to her lap. They'd never harmonized that well and he knew it.

"Thomas," she began. She could feel Spencer's fire-blue eyes on her, heard his words again. She shrugged, looked at the lyrics again. "All right."

"Good," he said. "Let's get to work."

♫♫♫

"I need to talk to you," Thomas said to Isabel as she snapped her guitar case closed.

She stood up. Everyone else had filed out but she wasn't afraid of Thomas. Not this time. She waited for him to say whatever he needed to say to make himself feel good about himself—jabs at her singing, insults about her playing. Instead of saying anything, though, he took a manila folder from his bag and slid it across the piano toward her. She looked at him as she caught it and opened it. Only a few words stood out on the paper before her.

Hereby terminated.
With immediate effect.
Rights of two songs retained.
Creative differences.
Settlement.

Isabel's hands shook. Each phrase on the paper be-

fore her was a stab in her solar plexus. She could feel
Thomas looking at her. She could feel the silence in the
room deep in her ears. When she looked up at him, he
raised his eyebrows. She could feel bile rise in her throat
and had to run across the hall to the bathroom. She barely
made it. When she came out of the bathroom after splashing water in her face, he was standing with his arms folded, looking at her as if she were vermin.

"This really shouldn't come as a surprise to you."

Isabel put a hand on her stomach. She still felt nauseous.

"Thomas," she began. "I know I hurt you. Spencer
and I both did, but—"

Thomas cut her off with a laugh. "Hurt me?" he repeated.

Isabel wanted to open her mouth to respond but felt
like she would throw up again if she did.

"Why no, Isabel," he said, coming closer, so close
that she back up against the wall. "You've inspired me.
You and Spencer. I've written some of the best songs
I've ever written over the past few months because of the
two of you. And now...well, I'm done. Through with
you. You've served your purpose."

He back away for a second to look her up and down.

"Besides, I asked you to do one little thing and you
couldn't do it."

She looked at him. She still couldn't say anything.

"You and Spencer," he said. "I told the two of you

that if you wanted to stay in my band, you would have to stay away from one another. And you didn't. All those little trysts at the hotels on the road, the times he came back to your apartment with you and stayed all night. Yeah, I know all about those times."

"Wait, were you following me?"

"I had to be sure you were upholding your end of the deal. And you weren't. So, here we are. Like I said, shouldn't be a surprise to you." He smiled now, his victory won. Then he came forward and kissed her violently. "Thank you, Isabel," he said. She felt like her lips were bruised. He turned and walked down the stairs. "Oh, and one more thing," he said, turning around halfway down. "Leave your key on the front table. Lock up on the way out. I'd appreciate it."

He was gone. Isabel watched him, her hand still on her stomach, her whole insides still twisted and nauseated. Jeez, what was wrong with her? She walked back and forth a few times. The place was so silent, so creepy at night when there was no one else in there. She grabbed her bag from the studio, remembering that damn termination notice. She was taking it to Spencer. Thomas wasn't getting away with this. She took her phone out and was still scrolling through her numbers to find Spencer's when she slipped on the top step on the stairway.

♫♫♫

The pinch of a needle in her arm. Light in her eyes. Floating, floating all around. Strangers calling out to her, asking if she could hear them. A stabbing in her ribs. Her lungs filling back up with air. She sucked in a breath. Pain. So much pain all over.

Spencer, she thought. *Where is he? I need him.*

Another stab in her abdomen. She managed to cry out. She could hear bustling around her and frantic voices as she floated down the hall again. Another blinding light.

Please, she thought again. *Make it stop. Make the pain stop.*

She forgot everything, even Spencer, as she said her silent prayer. And then, as she began to drift high and away again, it was finally answered.

♫♫♫

Isabel didn't know what day it was when she awoke. She was in a hospital bed, in a room of gray and white, save a television bolted in the corner. The only color came from the outside, the pine trees in the distance. The pain in her abdomen, back and legs had subsided to a dull ache, but she was still weak, almost too weak to press the button on the bed railing that had a nurse's cap on it.

She asked for water when a voice came through the intercom. Her throat was parched. An older nurse wearing scrubs, her gray hair pulled back in a tidy bun, brought her a cup of ice water and told her the doctor would be in in just a moment to talk with her.

He was an older man, with glasses and gray hair and was tall. He smiled at her briefly and greeted her by name as he looked at her chart for a long time. The fall had caused a broken rib and punctured lung, which they'd been able to repair, he'd said. But there was something else, too.

"What?" Isabel tried to sit up, but the ache was too strong. She felt something akin to a black cloak making its way over the room. "What is it?"

He hesitated and then moved around the bed and placed his hand over the IV over hers. "There's no easy way to tell you this. I'm afraid you've had a miscarriage."

Chapter 22

December 2016:

Spencer stared at her in the silence as she finished her story.

They had long since moved upstairs to his loft while the coffee shop opened up. They could hear patrons downstairs, people talking, laughing, the whir of the cappuccino machines, glasses and cups clanking. But they were silent, staring at one another.

"You—We—were pregnant," he said.

She nodded.

"Six weeks along," she said to the floor. "I didn't even know until he told me."

Spencer looked all around, taking in one breath after another fast, as if the room was losing air. He turned in a full circle before his eyes landed once again on Isabel. She didn't move. His blue eyes were fierce, angry, and when he walked toward her, taking the length between them in two strides, she instinctively stepped back. Spencer didn't stop. He took her face in his hands and began kissing her.

"I'm sorry," he said, over and over again.

She couldn't have pulled away from him if she wanted to. She didn't want to. She couldn't be far from him, not anymore, not now. She pushed against him, though not to get him away from her. She pushed him toward the direction of his bed as they ripped away one another's shirts, and then he lifted her so she could wrap her legs around him just before they collapsed on his bed. Their lovemaking was intense, angry, so unlike their other times. She poured the rage and sadness she'd felt toward him when he left, feeling it in her touch as she scratched him down his back, could feel the apology as he kissed her and pulled her closer and even closer to him. And when they were done, they fell asleep almost instantly, spent and exhausted.

Isabel didn't know what time it was when she woke up to Spencer running his finger up and down her spine, kissing her shoulder blade. She turned over to face him and he pushed her hair behind her ear. He smiled at her. She let him kiss her.

She loved him. She always would, she knew that. But he hadn't been there for her when she needed him most. He'd ignored her, disappeared. And she'd let him know how much that had hurt when she told him about the miscarriage, told him about laying there in that hospital bed alone, crying, trying over and over to call him and only getting his voicemail and giving up after the fifth day. She'd let him feel how hurt and angry she'd been.

But it wasn't enough. Laying here with him, feeling his touch, she knew that. He was the love of her life. But how could she be with him when she didn't know if he would do the same thing to her at any point in the future?

"What's wrong?" he asked.

Isabel could tell him. She wanted to. But she wanted more this one last moment with him before she left him for good. She shook her head, kissed him, and lay with him like that until she was sure he was sleeping. Then she slipped out from under the covers, dressed in her black turtleneck and jeans again, and left his loft for the studio.

It was only a little after eight. They didn't have to be at the studio until ten, but still Isabel walked quickly.

She was relieved to find the place empty and left the note with Thomas's name on it on the front table where he'd see it first thing when he came in. Then she turned to make her way back to Kat's. She didn't have a lot of time to get packed and get out of town.

Chapter 23

December 13, 2016:

*T*homas,
    I made a mistake. I thought I could do this, but being around you and Spencer again has proved to me that I can't. Too much happened six years ago, and seeing the two of you again only brought all of those memories back. You hurt me, and so did he, during a time when I needed him most. Don't ask me what I mean because I won't tell you. That's between him and me, and I've already told him. But I can't stay.

    I know I hurt you and, again, I am sorry for that. I love Spencer. I didn't choose to fall in love with him. I didn't plan it. And because of that, I am not apologizing for loving him. I'm just doing what I think is the best thing for all of us. I can't forget how he hurt me. You can't forgive either of us. And so I am doing the only thing I know to do. I'm leaving. I'm sorry it couldn't work out. I do hope you find the success, and the love, that you have always sought. Thank you, for everything.

Isabel

Thomas stood over the letter sitting before him on the conference table, reading over it again even though he had long since committed it to memory.

"Hey, man, we ready to go over those demos?" Greg asked, knocking on the doorframe. Thomas looked his way once before turning back, balling up the letter and throwing it in the trash.

"Get Spencer down here," he said.

Greg raised his eyebrows but turned to go back upstairs.

Spencer emerged in the doorway seconds later. He raised his eyebrows but other than that, the man looked hollow, confused. Thomas didn't answer. He paced, his arms crossed.

"What do you want, Thomas?"

Thomas studied him. And then he realized those were the first words Spencer had said since he arrived half an hour earlier. "Do you love her?"

"What?"

"Don't give me that. Do you love Isabel or not?"

Spencer scoffed. "You already know the answer to that."

"Say it," Thomas demanded. He had to hear it, otherwise he couldn't believe it.

"I love her! Okay? I love her, even though you forbid me to love her. Even though she, apparently, doesn't love me."

"What the hell does that mean?"

Spencer shook his head and looked away.

"How did you hurt her?"

"What?"

Thomas told him about the note.

"She said you hurt her. I want to know how."

Spencer stared at him for a long moment. "None of your damn business."

It was Thomas's turn to scoff as he looked up at the ceiling. "All right," he said finally. He ran his hands through his hair. "Go up to the roof."

"Why?"

Thomas didn't answer as he walked out the front door and took out his cell phone. Three calls to Isabel's line only unearthed her voicemail.

"Damn it," he said, replacing his phone in his pocket. He went back inside. "Hope!"

She was on her own phone. She told whoever it was to hold on a minute. "Yeah?"

"I need that address you tracked down for Isabel."

She flipped through her datebook and read it out to him. He entered it into his map finder on his phone, praying it wasn't that far, praying she was still there.

"One mile," he said, reading it. He looked up. "I'll be back. Tell everyone not to leave!"

"What are you doing?" she asked after him.

"Saving my band and…I don't know, doing the right thing, I guess."

He ran out the door to his car, started it up, and slammed it forward.

Be there, he thought, speeding down the little two lane road, passing a car on a double-yellow and running a stop light. *Be there. Be there. Be there. I'm almost getting myself killed here, doing the right damn thing for once in my life. Be there.*

He looked frantically all around at the house numbers before coming to the right one, a little blue one with red shutters. He didn't see Isabel's car.

Damn, he thought again, screeching to a halt and getting out, not bothering to close his own car door. He took the steps two at a time, panting as he banged on the door.

A tall, slim, older, attractive woman opened the door and put one hand on her hip. "What in the world are you doing banging on my front door like that at this hour?"

Thomas didn't bother apologizing. "I need to see Isabel Carson," he said.

"Well, just who in the hell are you?"

Thomas stopped, taken aback for just a moment.

"Uh, I'm Thomas. Isabel played with my band."

A certainty fell over the woman's features and she pursed her lips for a moment.

"Oh, right. Thomas."

He rolled his eyes. *Guess she told you all about me.* "Is she here?"

"I'm afraid you just missed her. She left about an hour ago."

"What? Where did she go?"

Thomas looked at his watch.

The woman glared at him. "*That* is none of your business. I'm sure if she wanted to give you that information she would have done it herself."

Thomas sighed and looked all around. Well, shit. What the hell was he supposed to do now? He turned back to the woman, the only one who could help him. "I'm just trying to make things right," he said, putting on his best innocent face.

She slit her eyes.

"I lied to her."

"A few times," the woman agreed.

"I want to apologize," he went on. "She can't leave like this. There's something she needs to know."

The woman looked at him a long moment before sighing and putting her index finger and thumb on the bridge of her nose. "Oh, I *so* shouldn't tell you this," she said. "But she's on her way back to Lilac Cove, is probably thirty or so miles out of Laurel Springs by now."

Thomas dropped, put his hands on his knees. Great. Just great.

"Sorry, hon," the woman said.

Thomas looked up. There was only one thing to do. He ran back down the steps while the woman still stood at the door watching him. He got into his car and again slammed the accelerator, speeding down the road. He'd speed all the way to Lilac Cove if he had to.

He didn't make it that far. At the first stoplight, he saw a familiar red Civic turning in front of him, and a familiar dark blonde head behind the wheel. He stopped, turning in his seat, to watch as the car turned down the road from which he'd emerged, and then he backed up, turned his car around, and sped off after it. He blew his horn, flashed his lights, and waved his hand out the window until the car stopped and, sure enough, Isabel got out.

"What the hell are you doing? You just about gave me a heart attack!" she said.

Thomas got out. "I tried calling you, but you didn't answer."

"Because I don't want to talk to you."

He ignored that. "I thought you were headed back to Lilac Cove."

"Forgot my makeup bag," she said. "What do you want, Thomas? Why did you stop me, acting like a maniac? What's wrong with you?"

"A lot," he admitted. "But we're not talking about me. You're not leaving here until I tell you something."

Chapter 24

February 2010:

Thomas flipped the last of the controls off in the studio and put on his jacket. He was just about to shut the lights off when he heard a knock. He turned to see Spencer leaning against the doorframe.

He took his time before addressing his friend. "What do you want?"

"All right if I talk to you a minute?"

Thomas scoffed. They'd barely talked since that day he'd found Spencer and Isabel in their love nest last month.

"I need a favor," Spencer said. He hadn't moved from the doorframe.

Thomas laughed out loud. "Well go ask Greg or Renee. Or one of your many conquests. Or go ask the only relative who gives a damn about you."

That ought to make him go away, Thomas thought.

But, it didn't. Spencer still stood there, hands in his pockets, looking at the floor. "It's about my uncle," he said.

Thomas pretended to shuffle some papers around, attempted to look too busy to deal with this.

"He had a heart attack a couple of days ago," Spencer continued. "He needs surgery and therapy afterward, and his insurance doesn't really cover much at all."

Thomas turned around and folded his arms, waiting for it.

"The bank turned me down for a loan, and—"

"How does this concern me?"

"It doesn't," Spencer began. "Not really. But if you loaned me the money—I know you have it from your parents—if you could loan me what I need to cover the surgery, I'll owe you big."

Thomas could feel a small smile. Well, the tables had certainly turned, hadn't they? He took his time before asking his next question. "Where is your uncle hospitalized?"

Spencer told him. Thomas took out his phone and called information. When he was connected with the hospital he asked after Spencer's uncle.

"Yes, he's due for surgery tomorrow," the reception-ist said sweetly.

"Thank you very much," Thomas said, smiling at Spencer as he hung up. "Well," he said. "Seems you're telling the truth."

Spencer was expressionless. He didn't ask again, but he waited. He loved his uncle. He couldn't lose him. He was, like Thomas had said, the only relative who gave a damn about him.

Thomas paced back and forth a couple of times. He could have anything he wanted. He could force Isabel to be with him if he wanted. He shook his head. No. Even he wouldn't do that. But he could do something else—

Thomas stopped in front of the window. "All right," he said.

"All right?" Spencer repeated.

"Yes. All right."

"Thank you, Thomas."

"Don't start celebrating just yet," Thomas said, turn-ing halfway so he could look him in the eye and see his reaction when he heard this next part. "There are a few things I need in return. Like you said, you would owe me big."

Spencer didn't move.

"First thing," Thomas said. He had to stop himself from rubbing his hands together. "You will leave the band only when I deem that your presence is no longer necessary. I will retain rights to all of the songs you wrote while in my band."

"Fine."

Oh was it, now? Thomas was going to get the best of this singer and songwriter and drain him dry.

"Second," Thomas said. "I want a song. A song detailing your relationship with Isabel."

"Already done," Spencer said. "The duet we do says it all."

"No, it doesn't," Thomas said. "That song paints you two in a romantic light. I want the gory details."

Spencer sighed. "Thomas."

"What are the odds of your uncle surviving without surgery?"

"Okay, fine!"

Thomas smiled. A nerve was pinched now. Time to go in for the kill.

"And while you are in my band, you and Isabel do not speak, do not lay eyes on each other, do not phone one another outside of the professional means. That means no contact outside of the studio or concerts. You understand?"

Spencer's jaw twitched.

"I know you two have been hooking up when you think no one's watching."

The disgust on Spencer's face was priceless. "All right."

"If she calls, you do not answer. There will be no

more sneaking between each other's hotel rooms—and most definitely no more sleeping together."

"You can't dictate how we feel about each other."

"Oh, I know that. And that's not what I'm asking if you listen closely. Besides, you two made that perfectly clear. You can love one another from afar all you want. But as long as you are working for me, you play like I tell you to. And if you want your uncle to survive, well, I strongly suggest you take me up on my offer."

Spencer turned his head to the ground and breathed deeply a few times before turning and slamming a fist into the wall. Thomas could hardly keep from laughing out loud.

"Fine," he said. "You have a deal."

"Great," Thomas said. "I'll have the lawyer draw up the contract tomorrow."

"Contract?"

"Gotta keep you to your word somehow."

Spencer sighed and turned to walk out.

"Oh, and one more thing," Thomas held up a finger, suddenly thinking of something. "You remember that Ben set us up with our cell plans when we started the band. All I have to do is ask him and I'll know exactly what numbers you've called, who's called you, how long you've talked—"

"I get the picture."

"Great. I'll expect you here at two to sign. And you're welcome."

Spencer didn't answer or turn around. But that was okay. Nothing could spoil Thomas's good mood now.

Chapter 25

December 13, 2016:

S till in the middle of the street, Isabel stood staring at Thomas as he finished his story.

"I don't believe you," she said.

"It's true," he said. "For once, I'm telling you the truth."

Isabel turned and put her hands on her head, clearly trying to wrap it around what he'd just told her. "Why?" she asked.

"You know why I did it," he said. "You just couldn't love me. So in my head I felt you needed to be punished. Both of you. Spencer gave me the perfect opportunity."

"No, I mean why are you telling me this now, after all these years?"

Thomas sighed and ran his hand through his hair. Well, he'd told nothing but the truth already today, may as well keep at it. "I'm desperate. If this next album doesn't do well, I'll be out on the street, playing for pennies. You know that. You and Spencer—the band doesn't work without the both of you."

Isabel looked at the ground and shook her head.

"I'll stay out of your way if you two really want to be together. I've been seeing someone lately, anyway. She's a stripper, so she's pretty great."

Isabel turned to him with a raised eyebrow, but still didn't say anything. Okay, so his attempt to lighten things hadn't worked. He opened his mouth to say he was sorry just as Isabel kicked his shin.

"Ow!" he said, grabbing his throbbing leg and hopping a few steps. Damn, that girl had a good right kick.

She jumped back when she did it, as if she were surprised at herself. "Sorry," she said. "That was for lying to me."

He half-laughed, rubbing his shin.

"But thank you," she said. "For telling me."

Thomas sighed. They stood for a silent moment until he couldn't stand it any longer. "So, can I tell my best songwriter and guitarist that the woman he loves is coming back?"

Isabel didn't look at him, and she didn't answer, either.

♫♫♫

How long did Thomas expect Spencer to hang out up here? It was getting cold. The sky was gray, and he could smell snow in the air. He shivered once and pushed his hands deep down into his pockets. His hand closed on his cell, and he pulled it out to look at it. Just as he thought. No missed calls. Not one. He must've called Isabel a thousand times that morning. She was gone. Just like the baby they'd never had a chance to hold and raise together. Gone. Spencer sighed. He'd blown it, all because of a choice he'd made long ago.

He closed his eyes to take in the cold air just one more time before he headed back in. When he opened them and turned, he saw her open the door to the roof. Neither moved for a moment as they stood, taking in the sight of each other until Isabel dropped the door handle. Then they both moved toward one another until they were in each other's arms.

Spencer took the back of her neck and kissed her, instantly and deep, parting her mouth with his own. Isabel no longer felt the cold she'd felt since leaving him, only the spark, the crackle of fire that his kiss still ignited in her nerves, and the steady warmth and safety of his strong arms around her, pulling and holding her closer, as if she might disappear if he didn't.

There was no cold, no one waiting for them. All of that faded away, and there was only the dizzying awareness of his arms around her, his face and warm breath against hers. He ended their kiss much slower than he began it, separating from her only little by little. He still touched his forehead to hers and kept her close to him as they caught their breath. When he spoke, it was in a raspy whisper: "Where did you think you were going?"

Isabel couldn't help but smile against his face. "I didn't know why," she began. "I didn't know why you never answered, never called. Thomas found me. He told me everything."

"I'm sorry," he said, turning his face into her neck, now. "I wanted to tell you. I should have told you."

"I'm sorry, too. For not giving you the chance." Isabel tucked her chin into his shoulder and looked out over the edge at the buildings in the distance. The sky was getting a little darker, the air icier.

"I have an idea," she said.

Spencer pulled back to look at her.

"Why don't we start again?"

He didn't say anything at first, so she continued with, "If it's okay with you."

When he still didn't say anything, she had a thought. Was that stupid? Unfair to ask? Maybe he didn't forgive her for walking out on him that morning.

She admitted that was a pretty crappy thing to do.

But then he smiled. "You love me or something?"

She cleared her throat and looked down before bringing her eyes up to look at him again, remembering. "Don't ask me questions you already know the answer to," she replied.

He nodded once. There was no music, but he put one arm around her and took her hand with the other. And, as he did, he caught sight of a silver ring with blue diamonds. He looked at it for a second and smiled before he brought her to him so they could dance just like they did on that balcony seven years earlier. He touched his forehead to hers. She turned her cheek so she could feel his with her own.

He sighed, his breath still warm against her face. "You know I'm not letting you go now that I have you back, right?"

Isabel hummed slightly in answer, but she knew she didn't have to say anything else.

As they danced close and without song under a white-gray sky sending down flakes of snow, she knew she didn't have to tell Spencer what he already knew.

About the Author

Tanya W. Newman was born and raised in Upstate South Carolina, where she discovered her love of writing and storytelling, a love that led to a Bachelor of Arts in English from University of South Carolina Upstate, and a Master of Arts in English from Clemson University.

Now married to her wonderful husband, Mark, for over ten years, Newman still resides in upstate South Carolina, where she sets many of her stories. When not writing or reading, she enjoys a good cup of coffee, movies (usually an action/adventure with a love story added in) or reruns of *The Golden Girls,* long walks, and spending time with her adorable son and daughter.

Visit her website at:
http://newmant720.wixsite.com/mysite.